THE UNEXPECTED
Connection

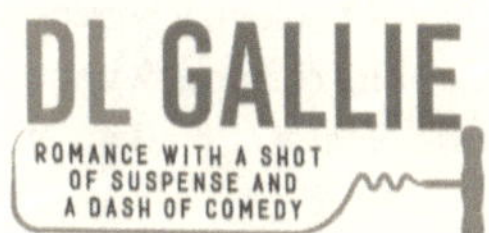

Can an unexpected connection change your life?

The Unexpected Connection
Book 4 in the Unexpected series

DL GALLIE

Published by DL Gallie Author

First published 24th November 2019

Edited by Karen Hrdlicka, Barren Acres Editing

Cover Design by Dana Leah of Designs by Dana

✹ Created with Vellum

Could an unexpected connection change your life?

They say good things come in twos but for Blair and Keeton, good things come in three.

For as long as they've known each other, their weekends were occasionally a triangle of kinky fun, but come Monday morning, it goes back to business as usual. That was until they meet Faith Robinson.

Faith unleashes something within them and love blooms in a spectacular way. When the numbers start to no longer add up, things get messy, especially when Faith's past catches up with her. Threatening to derail their new romance but their unexpected connection is what they need to overcome it all.

THE UNEXPECTED SERIES

The Unexpected Gift

The Unexpected Letter

The Unexpected Package

The Unexpected Connection

ALSO BY DL GALLIE

THE CASTAWAY GROVE COLLECTION

Love has arrived in the Grove

Oasis

Unequivocal Love

Five Words

Broken Rules - coming mid/late 2020

…and a few more as well.

THE LIQUOR CABINET SERIES

Liquor has never been so disturbingly saucy

Malt Me (Book 1)

Tequila Healing (Book 2)

Wine Not (Book 3)

The Final Shot (Book 4)

The Liquor Cabinet: Series boxset

STAND ALONES

Out of Nowhere

Antecedent

Seven Nights

Falling for Dr. Kelly, a Falling novel

Falling for Dr. Knight, a Falling novel - coming May 2020

Doc Steel - coming June 2020

The Dirty Dozen: Alpha edition

The Rule Breaker Anthology - coming soon

In the Dark of Night anthology (only available in paperback directly from me)

Titanic Tales, a charity anthology (no longer available)

Gone Coastal, a sizzling summer beach anthology (no longer available)

Leave Me Breathless: The Lilac Collection (no longer available)

To Jenny,
Thank you for asking for more Blair.
This ones for you.

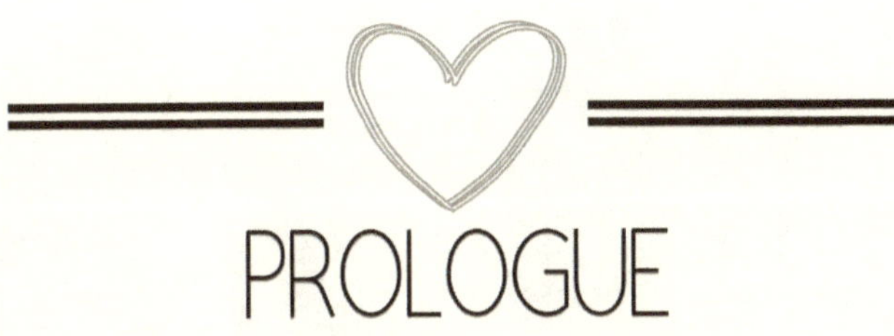

PROLOGUE

THERE WAS A POINT IN TIME WHEN WHAT WE DID WAS JUST FOR FUN. It was a night, or weekend, to let loose. Unleash our kinky inner inhibitions.

One weekend, it all changed when we met Faith Robinson, a copper-haired angel. This woman knocked us off-kilter and the dynamics changed between us.

This is the story of our unexpected connection.

FAITH

Flipping my head up, I shake my locks and stare at my reflection in the mirror. My lips lift into a grin, this color is off the charts bright. The flaming copper makes my blue eyes sparkle and seem bluer than usual. My parents, especially prim and proper Mom, would have a conniption if they could see me now. No longer do I wear pearls and pantsuits. No longer is my hair coiled and teased stiff with a heap of hairspray. No longer do I watch the clock, making sure I'm where I need to be, when I need to be. Now? Now my life is free of rules and timetables. My hair is mine to do as I please. For the first time in twenty-two years, I march to the beat of my own drum. I've never been happier…and I'm never going back.

Tonight, I'm heading to a new club that's opened up, Tingle, with my roommate, Eden Jennings. As soon as I met Eden, I knew I'd found my new best friend. Actually, she is my first 'real' friend, period! All the people I knew back home were more like acquaintances, and at the first opportunity, they'd stab you in the back if it meant they'd get ahead in life. From the moment we started talking, we clicked on every level and soon she *was* my best friend, roommate, my sister from another mister. Eden made the whole getting away from my family thing so much easier, I will be forever grateful for her taking me under her wing.

My parents, Fleur and Arnold Robinson-Bailey are what you call stuck-up assholes. They think they are better than everyone, especially Mother. People bow down to them and worship the ground they walk on. My mother is the mayor and my father is a top-notch lawyer. People in Collinsville think the sun shines out of their asses, what they don't realize is, behind closed doors they are two very different people. Me escaping their clutches was a long arduous process, which took months of scheming, plotting, and stashing money away for when I finally broke free.

I've been gone for six months now, and I'm surprised they haven't come looking for me, since by now they'd know I lied about what I was doing. I told them I was traveling through Europe to study the arts. That appeased Mother and I'm surprised she fell for it and let me 'organize' my trip myself. Daddy, on the other hand, I think he knew something was amiss but as usual, he didn't say or do anything. Daddy doesn't give a crap about much, as long as he has his scotch and his golf; he's a happy man.

Instead of going to Europe like I said, I caught a bus—Mother would never be caught dead on a bus—and headed to Chicago. Soon after I arrived, I found Eden, moved in with her, and the new me emerged. Carefree Faith has been unleashed and I'm never letting her go.

The only thing I miss about home is the warm weather. In Florida, cold days are few and far between; here it's cold for weeks, no months, at a time. At least I can rock kick-ass boots and the coats are to die for—I now have a coat addiction—hey, it's better than a coke addiction. I have a coat for each and every occasion; that's the only piece of advice from Mother I have retained and adhered to: *"You must have something unique for all occasions."*

Eden steps into my bedroom and whistles, pulling me from my memories and back into the present. "Holy hotness, woman. If I batted for the same team, I'd totally do you." Looking down, I smile. I'm wearing a silver strapless mini dress that hugs my body and doesn't leave much to the imagination. On my feet is a pair of sky-high ankle boots, but it's my new hair I love most. I've been getting braver and braver with each color, and this one is the most vibrant of them all. The copper color is intense, really intense. It makes my already bright eyes pop even more. Tonight, I left my hair wavy and my makeup light.

"Says the hot one," I counter as I take in Eden's outfit. She's wearing leather pants with a bright pink tube top and sky-high matte black heels that elongate her killer calves.

"You are totally hooking up tonight," she says, as she applies a pink lipstick that matches her top.

"Ohh, yes, please," I say. I haven't had many one-night stands, but without Mother breathing down my neck, it's easier to let loose and have some wild kinky fun…maybe even a three-some again, now that was a wild night. My insides quiver as I think back to that sexy time. I knew this side of me existed, but under Mother's rule, I was locked away. Now that I'm free of Mother's clutches, I'm running wild and letting the Faith I was always meant to be out of her gilded cage...I fucking love the new me.

"You and me both, sista. I need a good fuck and an amazing orgasm," she says, as she puckers her lips in the mirror, winking at me.

"Then let's do it," I cheerfully say, linking my arm with hers. We grab our things and head to Tingle...for a night I'll never forget.

BLAIR

Slipping on my shirt, I do up the buttons and smile to myself as I head out to the living room. I cannot wait to see what this feeling is.

"You okay, dude?" Keeton asks me as he hands me a beer.

"Yeah, I just have a feeling about tonight." He eyes me. "Not a bad a feeling, it's like...I can't really explain it. All I know, is tonight is going to be a night to remember."

"Let's hope it is a good feeling, we don't need any more shit in our lives."

"Ain't that the truth?" We clink our bottles together, and then he adds, "You sure you want to do it this weekend? It's been a pretty hectic week and all." Keet is referring to Amity Cuthel, now affectionately known as 'Whoreity.' The she-devil is back and causing trouble for Bennett once again, almost causing his new girlfriend, Stacey—who is perfect for him—to walk before they even get started.

"Yeah, I'm sure. We need a weekend to let loose and be carefree. And what better way than with a threesome?"

"Amen to that, brother." We clink our bottles in agreement.

We silently finish our beers, each of us contemplating the night ahead. Swallowing the last drop, I place my empty bottle on the coffee table and sit back on the sofa. Pulling my phone out of my pocket, I order our Uber for the evening. Keet grabs the empty bottles and drops them into the recycling.

"You ready, old man?" he teases, slapping me on the shoulder.

"Who you calling old, old man? You're older than me."

"Two years makes aaaall the difference," he exaggerates the sentence, flicking his head side to side in a playful teasing way.

Nonchantly, I shrug my shoulders. "When you are this side of thirty, all the years matter." Recently I turned thirty-one, and now I feel old and unsettled in life. I need a change but I don't know what. I'm sure it will come to be when I least expect it.

He laughs at me, and once again mocks me, "Ohh, it's so tough being thirty-one. Should we cancel the Uber and order you a walker? Or maybe a room in the local retirement village instead?"

"Fuck off, asshole."

My phone pings, letting me know the car is here. "It's go time," I say, raising my eyebrows at him. He shakes his head at me. We lock up and head downstairs, climbing into the waiting car. We silently make our way to Tingle, and the closer we get, that zinging feeling I felt earlier intensifies.

As soon as I step inside Tingle, that feeling slams into me like a freight train. My skin is buzzing as we walk deeper into the club…and then I see her. Tapping Keet on the shoulder, I nod toward the bar. He looks in the direction I nodded and his face immediately brightens. As usual, he and I are on the same page —we've found our girl. He and I have always been in sync when it comes to this arrangement, and it seems that tonight, we are once again on the same kinky page.

We change direction and walk toward her. My eyes take her in. Long copper hair hangs past her shoulders. Vivid blue eyes that pop in the dark lighting of the bar. Legs that go on and on and on—I can't wait to have them wrapped around my head. Gorgeous breasts, encased in a strapless sparkly number, that I imagine will fit in the palm of my hand perfectly. Cute button nose and plump perfect lips I cannot wait to kiss.

My eyes once again land on her gorgeous face and that's when she looks up. Our eyes meet across the room. The connection intense. Everything around me fades into the background. She smiles and it lights up her face. My and Keeton's steps fall into sync as we continue to make our way over to her. Her gaze darts between us, and from the expression on her face as she takes each of us in, it's almost like she knows we are a package deal. She lifts her eyebrows seductively at us and winks—yep, she knows. Her tongue darts out and she bites her bottom lip. It's the sexiest thing I have ever seen a woman do, and I get the sudden urge to bite it for her.

Keet steps in front of me and comes to a stop before her. "Hey," he nonchalantly says with a head nod, acting cool and calm. Me? I'm a bundle of excited nerves.

Her eyes flicking back and forth between us, she licks her bottom lip and then says, "Hey." The air surrounding the three of us is sizzling and crackling. Only two words have been spoken between the three of us and already it's getting steamy.

Sliding myself next to her, I lean back on the bar. My eyes

never leaving hers. Keet follows my action on the other side of her. She steps forward and my heart deflates at her dismissal of us, and then she turns to face us both. "That's better, now I can see you both. I'm Faith." She picks up her drink—bourbon, neat—and takes a sip. My eyes watch as she swallows.

"I'm Keeton, and this is Blair." He nods his head toward me, his voice deep and husky, indicating to me that, yes; he indeed does feel whatever this is between the three of us.

"Nice to meet you both." Her voice is soft yet rough and raspy at the same time. I've never been attracted to a woman like this before. It's making me nervous. "Can I buy you boys a drink?"

"Boys," I tease, "We are more than boys, Sweetness." I wink at her and grin, Keet shakes his head but from the amused smile on his face, he likes the banter between Faith and I. "How about *we* buy you a drink?" I ask, placing emphasis on the word we, reiterating again we are a package deal.

She raises her glass. "Thanks but I already have one."

Reaching out, I take the glass from her hand and throw back what was left. "It seems you need a drink now."

Keeton laughs and turns to the bartender ordering, "Three more, please."

The three of us silently stare at one another. The temperature around us quickly rising. The air no longer sizzling, it's crackling and ready to engulf us all. The moment is broken when the bartender places three tumblers in front of us. Faith, steps forward and takes her. "Bottoms up, boys." She lifts the glass to her lips and takes a sip. Her eyes lock on mine and I do the same. The amber liquid burns as it slides down my throat, pooling in my stomach, leaving my body warm and fuzzy.

"Sooo," Faith says, breaking the silence. "Shall we dance?"

Her eyes dart between the two of us again. "Sure, we'd love

to," I say, knowing that Keet will not be impressed, but when I look to him, he's grinning and totally up for dancing.

We follow her onto the dance floor and that's where our connection really heats up.

I'M ONE-HUNDRED-PERCENT SURE BLAIR AND I SAW HER AT THE exact same moment. A feeling I'd never felt before washed over me from head to toe. Looking to Blair, I see him nod in the same direction I was staring. With his head nod, I know that tonight everything is about to change.

With each step we take toward her, that feeling intensifies. Sure, Blair and I have done this many times before, but never have I ever felt like this. Without even speaking to her, I'm buzzing. The air around us is electrified. Everything around me is heightened as I focus on this copper-haired angel before us.

The sass from her mouth is sexy as fuck. I can't wait to have that mouth of hers wrapped around my cock or for her luscious lips to be pressed against mine. We share a drink with Faith, and now the three of us are heading to the dance floor. I don't know who suggested dancing, but if it means I can press my body against hers; then fuck yeah, I'll dance. I'm not really a dancer, dancing is more Blair's style, but when it comes to Faith, it seems I will do anything…even dance.

The club is packed but it's like everyone knows what's going on between us. They step apart, making way for us to walk through. We arrive in the center of the dance floor and the three of us fall into sync. Faith sandwiched between us. She's facing me, her back pressing into Blair's front. From the look on his face, she's brushing up against his dick with her ass. She's pushing herself into my chest, and her tits feel amazing pressed against me. Ohh how I wish we were naked, and I could feel her nipples pressing against my heated skin.

Gazing down, I see she's staring intently up at me. She's a good head length shorter than me, but we manage to fit together like three perfect puzzle pieces. She bites her lip, and I'm done for. Lowering my head down, I press my lips against hers. Fireworks explode within me when our lips press together. She has the softest lips I have ever had the pleasure of kissing. One kiss will never be enough, I'm addicted to her after one time.

All too soon, she breaks the connection with my lips, my hands track to her hips, holding her to me, still keeping us connected. Turning her head to Blair, she slides her hand behind his head and brings his lips to hers.

After kissing him, the three of us move to the beat of the music. The three of us swaying together: completely oblivious to the rest of the people in the club. The moment is broken when a drunken dick bumps into us, we take our cue and head back to the bar. Faith takes our hands, lacing her fingers with ours, and we walk toward her friend, who is grinning from ear to ear.

Faith comes to a stop in front of her. "I think I just got pregnant watching that," she declares as she pushes Faith to the side. "Hi, I'm Eden. That was hot and I'm so glad to see my girl here letting loose and having fun." She pauses and winks at us. "Some kinky fun."

"Nice to meet you, Eden, I'm Keeton and this is Blair." I nod my head to Blair, but he's lost in all that is Faith.

"Sooo," she drawls, "what are your intentions with my girl here?"

"Eden," Faith scoffs, whacking her in the arm. "Feel free to ignore her, I do."

"Pffft, you love me," Eden says, swinging her arm around Faith's shoulder. "But seriously, you hurt her, I hurt you."

Shaking my head, I smile. "I can guarantee you, Blair and I have no intentions of hurting her."

"Unless she wants us to," Blair adds with a wink. He wraps his arm around her waist, pulling her away from Eden.

Faith's eyes widen, swallowing deeply as she processes Blair's words, but I notice she snuggles into his side. Her gaze lifts to mine and a force overtakes my body, I push myself in-between Eden and her. Eden steps to the side, allowing me in.

"Catch ya later, babe," Eden singsongs, as she walks back-ward away from us. "And, guys, remember what I said." She lifts her hands, her index and middle finger making a 'V' and she flicks her wrist back and forth and mouths, 'I'm watching you.'

Faith laughs and her laugh is magical. "So that's my room-mate Eden."

"She seems—"

"The best," Faith interrupts. "I found her when I needed her, but now," she pauses for emphasis, "it seems I've found you two."

"Seems so," Blair states, "Should we get out of here?"

Faith nods, she laces her fingers with each of us and we exit the club. We climb into the back of a waiting taxi. As it pulls away from the curb, Blair give his address, and we make the journey back to his place for a night we will remember forever.

15

FAITH

As we eye fuck one another, I feel a finger brush along my upper arm, my skin tingling at his touch. Turning my head to the right, I see Blair hungrily staring at me. His green eyes carnal with lust...for me.

My tongue darts out and I lick my lip, gently biting. Blair swallows a groan. "So fucking hot," he whispers, his voice heads straight between my thighs and my clit throbs. Pressing my legs together, I try to sate the feeling but it only intensifies the sensation.

Warm breath on my left ear causes me to shiver. "I can't wait to help you with that throb," Keeton huskily says. My head swivels toward him.

"How did you know?" I breathlessly ask.

"I can read your body," he replies. Gently nipping my earlobe before whispering, "this spot right here," he trails his finger up and down my neck, "quivers when you're turned on. Your nipples are hard," he says, as he caresses my breast, gently massaging through my dress. He pinches my nipple and I gasp as my clit sparks to life. "And that pinch just caused your clit to explode like fireworks on the Fourth of July."

My mouth drops open in shock, how does he know this about my body already? "M-m-maybe," I stammer.

"There's no maybe, baby," Blair whispers. "Just you wait for the grand finale." He kisses below my earlobe. "It's going to be fucking phenomenal." He places his finger under my chin and turns my head toward him. He leans forward and presses his lips to mine, just as Keeton slides his hand up and down my side. Massaging my breast and laving my neck with nips and kisses.

My body has never felt alive like this before.

I'm not sure I'll survive a night with these two, but what a way to go. I whimper at the sensations coursing through my body. I've never felt pleasure this intense. I can only imagine what it will be like once the three of us are naked. At that thought, a moan slips free. I rock my hips to ease the throb, but that doesn't do a thing, if anything, is increases my need. My want. My desires. "Please," I murmur against Blair lips.

Keeton slides his hand down my stomach and cups my mound, my legs spread open on their own accord. He doesn't move his hand, he presses his palm down, kneading my clit as he continues to nibble and bite my neck. Blair fucks my mouth with his tongue. I'm just about to come when the car comes to a stop. "Sorry to interrupt," the driver says, his voice breathy and hoarse. "We're here."

Blair and Keeton pull away from me. I'm left a panting,

wanton mess. My clit throbbing. My whole body, from head to toe, thrumming with desire. "Come on, Sweetness," Blair says, offering me his hand as Keeton pays the driver.

Blair and I wait on the sidewalk for Keeton, as he's closing the door we hear the driver mumble, "Fucking lucky bastards."

My mouth drops open when it hits me what we were doing in the back of the taxi. Keeton laughs and Blair croons, "Soo fucking right we're lucky." He takes my hand and pulls me through the front gate and up the stairs to his place.

"Nice house."

"Thanks," Blair says. "My best friend lives down the street."

"You live down the street?" I ask Keeton.

He shakes his head. "No. He's referring to our other friend, and business partner, Bennett."

Nodding my head, I look over the house and smile. It's not the type of house I expected Blair to live in. I would have expected a bungalow, not this. He owns a beautiful brick Victorian house; I can't wait to see inside. Walking up the front stairs, he unlocks the door and steps aside to let me pass by. As I walk by, I run my finger across his chest, garnering a hiss from him. With a pep in my step, I sashay into the house.

The first thing I notice is the exposed brick throughout the bright and open plan layout—great for entertaining. A large eat-in kitchen with deck access. The living room overlooks a back courtyard. There's a gorgeous fireplace between the living and dining rooms. A massive L-shaped black leather couch faces the biggest TV I have ever seen.

A body appears behind me and he slides his hands around my waist, pulling me into his hard chest. His masculine smell envelops me and I think I know who it is. He bends down and nuzzles my ear, my assumptions are correct. I know those lips. "Keeton," I murmur as I drop my head back, resting it on his shoulder. I close my eyes as he continues to nip and suck my neck.

A finger traces along the top of my dress, dipping down and circling my nipple. Opening my eyes, I stare into emerald orbs that are full of desire and hunger, mirroring mine.

Keeton grabs the side zipper of my dress and drags it down, ever so slowly. Blair hooks his finger into the top of my dress, pulling it down and off my body. The shimmery material falls to the wooden floorboards, leaving me standing in nothing but my heels and lacy G-string.

"Fuck me," Blair growls, as his eyes roam over me. His stare heating my skin as it travels over my body.

From behind, Keeton cups my breasts; a moan slips out as he massages them. "What do you want?" he whispers, kissing my neck as he waits for my answer.

"Both of you," I whisper in reply, lifting my hand, I beckon Blair toward me. He steps in front of me and I push him sideways so he sits on the coffee table. Turning to Keeton, I press my lips to his. My tongue probing his lips for access. He opens and I slide my tongue in, like Blair did to me in the taxi, I fuck his mouth with my tongue. Sliding my arm around his neck, I grip his hair and gently tug.

I gasp against his lips when I feel Blair palming my ass cheeks. While kissing Keeton, he walked us closer to Blair, I was so lost in the kiss I didn't notice.

Blair slides his hand between my thighs. "You're soaked."

"Mmmhmpf," I murmur against Keeton's lips, as I continue to kiss him and wriggle my ass in Blair's face.

Blair runs his finger across the lace of my panties, and I moan into Keeton's mouth. I gasp when Blair tears—literally—my panties off. "Oops," he playfully says, as he drops the shredded material to the floor. He pushes a finger into me, then another, my torn panties forgotten as my body welcomes the intrusion of his fingers. If it wasn't for Keeton's arms wrapped around me, I would have fallen into a heap on the floor.

Blair continues to thrust his fingers into me from behind. Keeton slides his hand down my front and slides his finger across my clit. Back and forth he rubs my sensitive nub as Blair fucks me with his fingers. Reaching up and around, Blair squeezes my breast. Taking my nipple between his thumb and forefinger, he squeezes. That's the detonation I need and my orgasm viciously erupts. My head drops back and I scream as pleasure ripples through my body.

Two hands are great, four is fucking phenomenal.

Lifting my head up, I gaze into Keeton's eyes. He winks at me, bringing his fingers to his mouth, he licks my juices from them. "Mmmmm," he moans. Grabbing his cheeks in my palms, I slam my mouth to his; tasting myself on his lips releases something in me.

Breaking the connection with Keeton, I turn around to face Blair. Lowering my head, I press my lips to his. He grips my cheeks and fervently kisses me back. Keeton steps closer behind me and grips my hips, pressing his erection into my ass.

Looking over my shoulder, I hungrily whisper, "Fuck me, please."

BLAIR

HEARING HER ASK KEETON TO FUCK HER UNLEASHES SOMETHING inside of me. I've never felt a connection like this before, and I cannot wait to see what happens next.

From behind, I hear Keeton, "With pleasure." He pauses. "But first, suck his cock."

She turns to face me; with a sexy wink she mimics Keet's reply. "With pleasure," she purrs.

Before I register what's happening, she drops to her knees and reaches forward. Popping the button open, she makes quick work of my zipper. Gripping the top of my jeans, she begins to slide them and my briefs down. Lifting my ass up, she pulls them down and off me. Tossing them to the side. Her eyes are locked on my cock, as she pushes my shirt up and out of the way. She licks her lips, again gently biting the plump pillow of her bottom lip. My cock is harder than steel right now, the tip glistening with precum.

Finally, she lowers her head toward my cock. Her tongue darts out and she swipes it over the tip. "Fuuuuck," I growl, and then she takes my cock into her mouth and sucks. "Fuuuuck," I moan again, Keeton scoffs. Flipping him the bird, I slide my fingers into her hair and guide her head up and down my cock.

Keeton pushes the coffee table back and slides in behind her. His cock sheathed with a condom; he grips her hips and presses his cock into her from behind. She moans around my cock, the vibration and warmth of her mouth feels amazing.

The three of us thrust as one.

My dick into her mouth, Keeton's cock into her pussy.

And repeat, over and over.

Dick into mouth. Cock into pussy.

Moan.

Groan.

It's pure ecstasy. I'm high on lust and never want to come down.

"Fuuuuck," Keeton growls, "Your pussy was made for my cock."

"And your mouth was made for mine."

Keeton picks up his pace. I can tell he's close by the way he's breathing, then all of a sudden, she grips my balls and presses my perineum and it sparks my orgasm immediately. Incoherent mumbles slip from my mouth as I come down her throat. She sucks every last drop. My cock slips from her mouth and she screams, "Yeeeeeesssssss!" Throwing her head back, she tumbles over the edge in sync with Keeton, their grunts and moans filling the room as they each give in to the pleasure.

Keeton leans down and kisses her upside down from behind,

I watch as the two of them kiss. Their bodies tight and rigid. As they continue to kiss, their bodies relax and they come down from their orgasmic high.

Breaking the connection, Keeton looks to me and winks. Faith lifts her head back upright and stares at me. Her cheeks are rosy from her release. The room is silent, except for the heavy breathing emitting from the three of us.

She breaks the silence when she says, "Hi."

That one word causes me to laugh, then then three of us are chuckling.

Keeton steps back and removes the condom. Dropping it onto the coffee table, he takes a seat on the table next to me. Faith is still on her knees between my thighs. She flicks her gaze between us, her eyes darkening with hunger. "I think we've unleashed a sex monster," I playfully tease.

She slaps my thigh. "Takes one to know one."

"She's got you there, Blair," Keeton agrees.

Shrugging my shoulders, I stand up, reach down, and pick her up. Spinning around, I sit on the sofa, placing her next to me. Keet joins us and she leans into my side, shifting around—her legs across Keeton's lap—and snuggles in as I drape my arm across her stomach.

Keeton and I gently stroke her skin. I run my finger in circles on her stomach, brushing the bottom of her breasts. Keeton caresses her legs. A moan slips from her lips when I notice Keeton is stroking between her thighs. She spreads her legs, giving him easier access to her pussy. Leaning down, I nuzzle her neck and begin to fondle her breasts. The air sizzling once again. Desire running through our veins.

Sheathing my cock with a condom, she shuffles onto my lap. Our bodies move as one as she sinks herself down onto my cock, her back to my front. Keeton stands up and steps in front of us.

She reaches out and strokes his cock. Leaning forward she slides it into her mouth.

The three of us moan as we once again let the pleasure envelop us. Never have I felt a connection this intense with someone in the past. Sure, Keeton and I have done this many times before, but it's always been a little awkward, trying to find the perfect fit for everyone involved, but with Faith, it's like she was made for us. We work in harmony together, with little thought or effort into the logistics of being a threesome. We bring each other immense pleasure. We gel together perfectly, and I don't think just tonight is going to be enough. One weekend is not going to be enough. There's a connection between the three of us that's too hard to ignore, I just hope in the light of the morning, I still feel like this.

KEETON

WALKING INTO THE CLUB.

Spotting the copper-haired angel.

Dancing with said angel.

Blair and I leaving with said angel.

A dirty sexy taxi ride.

An unbelievable sexy evening in Blair's living room.

A steamy—and not because of the water temperature—shower.

Collapsing into bed. Our legs twining together. Snuggling together.

Sleeping like a baby.

What an evening.

Faith wriggles in her sleep, her ass brushing against my cock. My cock likes the feeling of her naked ass rubbing against it. It immediately hardens. She circles her hips and when she does this, I know she's awake. Leaning toward her, I nuzzle her neck. "Morning."

She rolls over to face me and my cock misses the feeling of her cheeks pressed against it, that is until she rests her hand on my chest and presses her lips to mine. Sliding her arm around me, she pulls me into her. Her breasts and nipples pressing into me, just like I wanted last night while dancing with her at Tingle. I deepen the kiss and slip my tongue into her mouth. Slipping her hand between us, she grips my cock and begins to stroke me. A moan slips from her lips and I realize Blair has his hand between her thighs, stroking her. Her grip tightens on my shaft, it's bordering on painful when she suddenly breaks our kiss. She slides down the bed and wraps her lips around me. *Fuck me!* I moan when she gently rakes her teeth up my shaft, sucking on the head before repeating the process.

Blair is on his knees beside her, his hand still between her legs and his other hand is stroking himself. The air fills with our moans and groans as we bring each other to climax. One after the other, like a chain reaction we each peak and tumble over the orgasmic cliff.

We collapse onto the bed, panting from our early morning workout. No one says anything, our heavy breathing the only sound in the room.

"Now that's a way to wake up," Blair says, breaking the silence.

"Mmmhmpf," I say and Faith laughs, her laugh is magical.

She sits up, spins around, and crosses her legs. Her gaze drifts between Blair and me. "Can I just say, last night, was the best night of my life."

"Agreed," I say in reply.

"Fuck yeah," Blair eagerly affirms.

Then it's silent again. The three of us staring at one another, the awkwardness of the morning after has finally arrived. "Sooo, I'm gonna go," Faith says as she climbs over me. Naked as the day she was born, she walks out into the living room to where her clothes are.

Looking to Blair, he shrugs but his eyes tell me everything; he doesn't want her to go either. I climb out of bed while Blair—Mr. Gung Ho himself—jumps, literally, off the mattress. He rounds the end and his foot gets caught in the duvet he kicked to the floor. He goes down in a heap, his legs kicking to free the material from his feet and legs. On his way down, his head hits the dresser. This causes a photo frame to fall off. It hits the wall and smashes on the tiles in the en suite bathroom with a loud bang. Glass and the frame shatter into a heap of tiny pieces.

"Shit balls!" he shouts as he sits up, rubbing his head where it connected with the dresser.

At the sound of the commotion, Faith comes rushing into the room. "What the hell?" Her eyes look from me to Blair on the carpet. I'm now sitting on the end of the bed, laughing my ass off. Blair flips me the bird as Faith squats down, giving me a stunning view of her ass that's now covered by her sparkly dress from last night. "What happened? Are you okay?" she asks Blair.

Blair nods. "I'm fine. My foot got caught and I went down like a sack of potatoes."

This causes Faith to laugh. She loses her balance and she falls toward Blair. She tries to maneuver out of the way so she doesn't hit him, but in doing so, her elbow connects with his family jewels.

His eye pop wide open and he groans, "Fuuuuck," as he covers his nuts, trying to soothe them. Again, I burst out laughing. "You're an asshole," he snarls through gritted teeth.

"Oh My God, I'm so sorry," Faith says, as she sits up. She

reaches out to Blair, cupping his cheek. Their eyes connect, and from where I'm sitting on the end of the bed, I can feel the connection and spark between them. The air is electrified.

The two of them stare at one another, the moment is intense but at the same time, it's perfect. Her thumb brushes along his cheek. "Are you okay?"

He nods. "Yeah, I'm okay."

Standing up, I walk over to them. Reaching out, I offer Blair a hand. He grips my hand and I pull him up. We both turn and face Faith, she's sitting on her knees, staring up at us. Her gaze flicks between Blair and me, even though we are both naked, her eyes are locked on our faces.

The stare is heated.

It's intense.

It's carnal.

The connection between the three of us is strong.

Her tongue darts out and she licks her lips. My eyes track her tongue's path and Blair croons, "Fuck, I love when you do that."

Reaching down, I rub my finger over her lip. She inhales deeply as I cup her cheek, and she leans into my hand.

The air around us is crackling.

She reaches up pressing her hand up to mine. When her palm connects with my skin, an electrical current zaps up my arm, bringing my body to life. She gasps, she felt it too.

Blair threads his fingers into her hair, cupping her head in his palm. She turns her attention to him and with her other hand, she places it over his. His eyes widen when she touches him. I guess he felt the spark that I too felt, moments ago, when she touched me.

She pushes herself up. The three of us standing together. Our breathing the only sound in the room. Never has a moment felt so perfect before. None of us utter a word, our stares telling each other everything.

Faith breaks the moment when she steps back. Blair and my hands holding their place in the air, until she laces her fingers with each of us. She steps between us and walks toward the bed. She drops our hands and sits on the end, she taps the mattress either side of her, and then she utters six words that generally mean disaster, "I think we need to talk."

FAITH

"I THINK WE NEED TO TALK." MY HEART IS RACING AS I UTTER THOSE words. "It's not a bad talk, it's just, I, umm, ahh, I think…" I trail off as my nerves kick in. My gaze dropping to the floor.

"Think what?" Keeton says, as he sits next to me, resting his palm on my thigh. My skin heats at the connection. Blair sits on my other side; being sandwiched between the two of them instantly calms me.

Raising my head, I look between them and a feeling of peace washes over me. Taking a deep breath, I decide to go for it. "I think. No, I want to see where this goes. Call me crazy, but last night was fucking amazing. The three of us have this connection that was so unexpected, and I want to explore it. I've never felt like this before. I know it's crazy, since I only met you both less that twenty-four hours ago, but I—"

"Yes," they both say at once, shocking me.

"We feel it too," Blair says. I look to Keeton and he's nodding his head. "As you probably guessed, Keet and I have done this before but never like last night, or this morning. The three of us mesh, and I'm pretty sure we will get along like a house on fire, surely with the sexual chemistry there will be an emotional connection as well."

My head nods as I listen to him speak. I take in each and every word that comes out of his mouth, and I can't believe that he, they both, feel what I feel. It's only been a short period of time, and we've hardly spoken but when we have, it hasn't been awkward or forced.

Looking to Keeton, I notice he hasn't said anything, but he's still gripping my thigh and running this thumb gently back and forth.

"Keet?" I softly ask. "You're quiet, what do you feel and think about all of this?"

"I don't need to say anything because you both have expressed what I feel."

It's come to my attention, as Keeton speaks now, he's the reserved and in control one. Whereas, Blair is the wild, crazy, I-don't-give-a-fuck-what-people-think one. He's the polar opposite to Keet but at the same time, he's what Keet needs to come out of his shell, and Keet is who Blair needs so he doesn't end up in jail, or worse. Together, they are the complete package, and now, they are my package.

Blair drops to the floor in front of me, taking my hands in his. "Faith, let's do this."

Keeton reaches over and places his hands on top of ours, he squeezes them and winks. "You in, Faith?"

Nodding my head, I smile. "Yeah, I'm in."

Keeton wraps his arm around my shoulder, pulling me into his side. He kisses my temple and with that one gesture, I know he's all-in. Blair brings my hand to his lips and kisses my knuckles.

"Let's eat," Blair says, as he looks between us.

My thighs spread on their own accord. I drop to the mattress and wait for his mouth to connect with my pussy, but he surprises me and presses them back together, reaching for my hand, and pulling me back into a sitting position. "As much as I'd love to have you for breakfast, I meant real food." He pauses and stares at me, his gaze setting my insides ablaze with desire and heating my skin. "We will need ALL the energy for what I have in mind for us later."

"Ohh," I say, my cheeks darkening with embarrassment and my insides quivering with want and need.

"Babe, never be embarrassed to ask for what you want," Keeton croons. He glances to Blair and a look passes between them, and then he turns to me and winks. "I think we have time for a quick snack before breakfast."

Before I can process his words, I'm pushed onto my back. Keeton presses his lips to mine and Blair presses his face between my thighs. My legs spread open on their own again, giving Blair greater access. Keeton kisses down my neck, across my collarbone and down to my breasts. He massages them and squeezes, taking my nipple into his mouth, sucking and nipping.

A guttural moan breaks free. My breasts have always been sensitive but Keeton, fuck, he knows how to suck a tit. Combine that with Blair's tongue and his fingers in my pussy, and I'm a quivering wanton mess. Just as I'm about to tumble over edge, they both stop. Lifting my head, I see them swapping positions.

Keeton is now between my legs, and he picks up right where Blair left off. Blair lies beside me and brushes a tendril of hair behind my ear. "Hi," he whispers before pressing his lips to mine. I can taste my arousal on his lips. I smile into our kiss as the pressure begins to simmer within again.

Blair and I kiss. I slide my fingers into his hair and increase the pressure when I feel Keeton press his finger against my asshole. My body tenses for a second, and then something washes over me and I relax. He slips the tip of his finger in and I see every color of the rainbow as my orgasm explodes like fireworks on the Fourth of July. My body tingles from the top of my head to the tip of my toes.

Each time with these two is better than the last.

My body relaxes as the last tremble subsides. If I weren't lying down, I'd collapse into a heap. Keeton climbs onto the bed on my other side. Breaking the connection of my lips with Blair's, I look to Keet, his chin is glistening with my arousal. Lifting my hand, I wipe his lip and bring my finger to my mouth and slip it inside, sucking off my juices. "MMMM," I whisper-moan.

Keet shakes his head and grins at me. "You are a sassy minx. If I wasn't starving, I'd straddle you and fuck you." I smirk at him. "But you'd totally love that punishment so I'm going to make you wait." He climbs off the bed. "Let's go eat."

Standing up, I pull my dress down, "Do you think we could swing by my place, so I can grab a new pair of panties and a change of clothes?"

"Nope," Blair says, as he walks into his closet. He returns with a charcoal grey dress shirt and a belt. He hands them to me. "You can wear this." I take the items from him. "I like you not having any panties on," he kisses my temple, smirking, "it means I can do this." He slides his hand between my thighs and rubs my clit. Removing his hand, he licks his finger. "Come on, get dressed. I'm starved."

With that, he and Keeton leave me in his bedroom. The two of them must have gotten dressed while I was off in la-la land.

Lifting my dress over my head, I slip on the shirt, roll the sleeves up to my elbows, and wrap the belt around my waist. Glancing at my reflection in the freestanding mirror in the corner, I grin. This outfit looks awesome. Running my fingers through my hair, I unknot what I can. Then I shake my hands and mess it up, giving it some body. Once I'm happy, I step into the living room, grab my shoes, and meet the guys who are standing by the island counter.

"Fuck me," Blair says, "you wear that shirt better than I do."

My cheeks darken at his compliment, then Keeton says, "You were sexy in that sparkly number last night but this, fuck, I have no words. You are a divine goddess, Faith." I swallow at his words. "Now let's go eat so we can get back here, and we can worship every inch of your delectable body."

Once again, his words cause my body to erupt in goose-bumps. Before I can reply, he takes my hand and drags me into the garage. We climb into Blair's car and head off to breakfast.

When we return, we do exactly as they promised. They worshiped every inch of my body. No part of me was left untouched. I now ache in the most delicious way and I cannot wait to feel like this again.

BLAIR

…Three weeks later

THE LAST THREE WEEKS WITH FAITH HAVE BEEN AMAZING. THE three of us connect like we are meant to be, and I'm not just talking about in the bedroom. Sure, we steam up the sheets whenever we can, but we also connect on an emotional level. In amongst all the kinky wild sexy times, we chat and laugh or silently watch a show on Netflix. It's never awkward, what we have is the epitome of perfection. Keeton, Faith, and I have the ultimate connection, and I will do whatever it takes to protect what we have. I'm never letting it go.

Keet and I have always hidden our kinky side, but I'm at the point where I don't want to hide anymore. I want to shout from the rooftops that we have an amazing girl and I'm falling for her, but it's always been a secret. I'm not sure how Bennett would take it. Last week, when Stacey came by with dinner, and we heard about her friend and the kinda, sorta, not really a three-some with the brother and dead fiancé/baby daddy, it left the atmosphere weird between Keet and me. We didn't get a chance to discuss it, but I'm guessing all is okay, because when we saw Faith that following weekend, it was just as hot as always.

We are on our way to Faith's place now. We are picking her up and she's going to spend the weekend with us. Then we are all going out to dinner and then back to Keet's place for a steamy hot night—gotta do something to warm up—since winter is kicking our ass this year.

Dinner is a quiet affair, Faith is not her usual self. She was excited to see us when we arrived, but something is amiss. Her mind is all over the place, she is deep in thought most of the evening and quiet, it's not like her at all. Hell, she barely laughed at my jokes and normally she laughs all the time. Keet even senses that something is off.

We wrap up dinner, declining dessert, and head back to Keet's place. She's even quieter on the car trip, I didn't think that was possible with how meek she has been all evening. Her behavior is worrying me. Is she sick of us? Does she want to end what we have? All these questions and scenarios run through my mind. I really hope she's not tired of us, we haven't even begun to show her what we feel. Keet and I haven't discussed it, but I'm one-hundred-percent sure he feels what I feel, and I know, deep down Faith does too.

We enter Keet's house and he heads to the kitchen to grab a bottle of wine. While he opens it and pours us each a glass, Faith and I head into the living room and take a seat on the sofa. She snuggles into my side, but I can feel apprehension radiating around her.

From behind us, Keet hands us each a glass before heading back to grab his own and the bottle of wine. He places the bottle on the coffee table and sits next to us. We all clink our glasses together in a silent toast.

Faith takes a sip and moans as the fruity tannins hit her taste buds, she relaxes a little and then takes a deep breath. "Can I ask you guys a question?" she hesitantly asks, her voice nervous, not at all confident like she usually is. I notice her hand is shaking a little as she brings her wine glass to her mouth, taking another sip, this one much larger than the first sip.

"Sure," Keet says, his eyes flick over to me, and I can see he feels the unease that I do too.

"Are you guys seeing someone else too?"

Her question shocks both of us. "No," Keet and I say in unison. Each of us shaking our heads to emphasize the no.

"Why do you ask?" I question, reaching over, I grab her hand and squeeze it reassuringly, resting our joined hands on my thigh. This gesture doesn't ease the anguish on her face.

"It's…nothing. It's silly," she offers, with a smile that's faker than Pamela Anderson's tits.

"Want to try again, Sweetness?" Keet says, as he takes a seat on the coffee table across from both of us. He takes the wine glass from her trembling hands and places it next to him.

Her gaze flicks between us. "I've seen you both with another woman on separate occasions. The same woman. I thought maybe you are also doing this with someone else."

My eyes scrunch in confusion, as do Keet's.

"Can you describe this woman?" I ask.

"Pretty. Dark hair. Tall. Killer legs. Great smile."

"Is she talking about Stacey?" I ask Keet.

He shrugs in a 'beats me' kinda way. I think about all the women that we know, and Stacey is the only one who comes to mind, so I presume it's her. "Where have you seen her with us?" I ask, hoping to get more information to figure this out.

"Near your office."

We both nod. "Faith, babe, that's Stacey, Bennett's girlfriend," I say, lifting my hand to cup her cheek. I feel the tension leave her body at our answer. It's like a wave of relief washes over her as she nuzzles into my palm.

"Aww, were you jealous, Sweetness?" I tease, removing my hand from her cheek and poking her in the ribs.

"No," she snaps in reply. I purse my lips and watch her. "Okay, yes, I was jealous. I like having you two to myself. I don't want to share."

"We don't want to share you with anyone else either," Keet confirms, he drops to his knees and crawls between her thighs, resting his palms on her knees. He lowers his head and kisses her thigh. "Do we need to show you…" Kiss…"remind you…" Kiss…"of how good we are together?"

She nods with a grin, a sexy as fuck grin.

"Faith, babe," I whisper, nuzzling her earlobe, gently nipping with my teeth. "We are going to show you how much you mean to us. We don't need, or want anyone but you."

"Okay," she breathlessly whispers, her head dropping back, elongating her perfect neck. Gently I run the tip of my finger down the taut skin, pulling her top down as I slide my digits down the valley of her breasts. Letting the material go, it flicks back into place. Gripping the hem of her top, I lift it over her head, leaving her in the jeans and bra.

Cupping her perfect breasts in my palms, I gently massage. She moans when Keet climbs onto the couch next to her. He presses his lips to hers as I push down the cup of her bra and take her perfectly pink nipple into my mouth. She cries out in pleasure, as we each continue to our assault on her mouth and breast.

Keet begins kissing down her neck, toward her other breast. She lifts her hands, raking her fingers through my hair before she pushes gently on my head, she wants me between her thighs but I'm not letting her get what she wants so easily. "What do you want, baby?" As say it, I massage her breast, my eyes locked on hers.

"Your mouth," she whimpers.

"You have my mouth," I say, before I suck on her breast, gently nipping her nipple before letting it pop free.

"Tell us what you want," Keet growls.

"I want a cock in my mouth and another in my pussy," she purrs, her eyes flicking between the two of us.

Looking to Keet, I shrug. "Should we give her what she wants?"

He nods. "Ab-so-fucking-lutely."

He stands up and walks to the end of the sofa, unbuttoning his jeans as he goes. Stepping out, he kicks them and his briefs to the side. Gripping his cock, he strokes up and down as Faith lies back on the couch, her head hanging off the end. Keet lowers to his knees and feeds his cock to her. I make quick work removing her clothing. First, I strip off her jeans and panties before removing mine. Sliding a condom on, I settle between her thighs and give her what she wants; my cock in her pussy and Keet's cock in her mouth.

Keet thrusts his cock in and out of her mouth while I slide my cock between her thighs. She's wet and ready for me. I thrust in and out of her, in sync with Keet sliding his cock in and out of her mouth. Like always, the three of us come in unison. Each of us moaning in delight as our bodies succumb to the pleasure.

Keet picks a spent Faith up and we head into the bedroom.

We blissfully fall asleep, entwined together, our connection now stronger than ever before.

FAITH

THE EVENTS OF THE LAST FEW WEEKS ARE PLAYING ON A LOOP IN MY mind. I find myself smiling and my insides buzzing, these guys do things to me, mentally and physically. I have no control over how I feel, but I don't ever want to stop feeling like this. I never imagined meeting anyone, let alone two gorgeous men, but here I am—sandwiched between them—my new favorite spot to be, by the way. The sexual and emotional connection I have with Blair and Keeton is nothing like I've experienced before. Sure, I've previously had the odd threesome but it was always a wham-bam-thank-you-ma'am kind of thing. This, this is different in so many ways. It's not just us getting dirty between the sheets, we also talk and laugh, I genuinely love spending time with them. Whether it's together as three or one-on-one with them.

We've connected on the deepest of deep levels, really getting to know one another. Listening when something is wrong. Offering advice when asked. Opening up on the inside and sharing our innermost and darkest secrets. Well mostly, I'm still hiding who I really am but apart from that little-big secret everything is open and honest with us. In such a short amount of time, I feel like I've known them forever.

I've discovered even though Blair is carefree and goofy, underneath it all is a sweet and caring guy. And Keeton, Mr. Serious and Quiet, is actually pretty funny and impassioned. They bring out the best in me, they bring out the real me. I'm glad Eden dragged me to Tingle the other weekend, because it led me to Blair and Keeton.

The three of us connect on every level, I've never felt like this with a partner before, but as they say, 'when you meet the one nothing else matters.' In my case, 'it's when you meet the two,' maybe that's why it's so intense; there's three of us. I'm falling for these guys hook, line, and sinker...I just hope my past doesn't ruin my newfound happiness.

After spending the weekend with the guys, I head home early Monday morning. Eden and I are like ships in the night, passing one another and we keep missing each other. On Tuesday when I head out for the day, I leave her a note saying: I'll pick up dinner tonight. On my way home, I stop in at Jewel Osco and grab all the ingredients for tacos, since it's Taco Tuesday. From the moment I moved in, Eden and I have a standing date each Tuesday—tacos and Coronas.

From outside in the hall, I hear music playing when I arrive and know Eden is home. Kicking the door shut behind me, I walk inside and singsong, "Honey, I'm home."

"Well, well, well, look who decided to come home," she teases, as I walk into the kitchen to meet her. She takes the shopping bags from me and begins unpacking. Placing the beers in the fridge, I grab two out. Flipping off the caps, I hand one to her. "To Taco Tuesday," I toast.

"Taco Tuesday," she says in reply, as she taps her bottle with mine.

We each take a sip and let the yeasty goodness soak into our souls. We fall in sync and begin preparing dinner. Eden chops up the vegetables and I prepare the meat. While it simmers, we take our beers out onto the balcony and stare at the sunset: the sky already ablaze with oranges and purples. The bright orb of the sun just peeking over the horizon, but soon it's dark, the city lights illuminating the night sky.

"So," Eden asks, "how are you?"

"Good," I offer.

"Good? Really? That's all I get?" I look to her and shrug, "You've been absent for nearly three weeks now. You are beaming with that 'I get fucked on a regular basis' glow, and all I get is good? Nope, nah, uh, I want all the kinky, sexy details."

"It's really good." She glares at me and I laugh. "I can't explain it, Eden. It's really good, like really, really, greatly good. I'm genuinely good. Seriously, everything is—"

"Good," she interrupts with a grin. "It's nice to see you smiling, like really smiling. It's like you are a different person since meeting them. I think the real Faith Robinson has arrived." Eden knows a little of my past, hearing her confirm what I'm feeling, that the real 'me' is here, feels good. I was lost for so long, but now I've found happy me. I don't ever want to stop feeling like this.

"You're right, Eden, I think I've finally found me, the real me, and it's all because of them. They freed me from the invisible chains I had myself wrapped up in. For the first time in twenty-two years, I'm not anxious or worried about pleasing everyone. I'm looking out for me and it feels great." I grin at her, using the word great again. "Keet and Blair treat me like a princess, but they don't keep me on a pedestal. I'm their equal. They genuinely care what I think and feel. My opinion and feelings matter."

"Sounds like you're in love."

Shaking my head I smile. "Not in love but definitely falling." That's the first time I've voiced aloud my true feelings for Blair and Keet. It feels great—there's that word again—to tell someone. Looking to Eden, I see she's smiling back at me. She's happy for me. I know that Mother and Daddy wouldn't be happy, and Trenton, well he doesn't give a fuck about anyone but himself. You'd think after I saved his life when we were little he'd be a bit more loving and grateful toward me.

Taking a sip of beer, I realize leaving and coming to Chicago was the best decision, not only did I meet Keet and Blair, but I met Eden. She's the sister I always wanted and so much more. A tear escapes, I quickly wipe it away but eagle-eyed Eden sees. "What's with the waterworks?"

"It's one tear."

"Okay, what's with the one tear?"

"I'm happy I have you in my life. I'm glad to be free of Mother and Daddy and Trenton, but most of all, I finally feel like I know who Faith Robison-Ba—is." I stop myself from using my full name, that's something I haven't shared with anyone since arriving here.

"She's a sexy as hell badass bitch who's screwing two fine as fuck men." I laugh at her crassness but she's right: I am a badass bitch who is screwing two fine as fuck men.

"Thank you," I say.

"Why are you thanking me?"

"Because you took me in. You gave me a home. A friend. You gave me my life back, Eden. I will forever be grateful for that."

"Dammit, you bitch," she sniffles, "now I'm crying, and more than one fucking tear too." We both laugh. "I'm happy to have met you too. Now, no more of this pussyness. It's Taco Tuesday and I think tonight, margaritas are in order. We need to celebrate finding each other, and I'm hoping if I get you drunk enough, you'll share all the kinky sexy details with me."

"Bring it on...but my lips will remain zipped." I mime zipping my lips. "What happens in kinky club—stays in kinky club."

"Challenge accepted."

We both laugh, as we head into the kitchen to whip up our first batch of margaritas.

Eden and I have a fantabulous night together, and much to her disgust, my lips remain sealed. I don't share about what transpires between the sheets with the three of us.

The next morning, we are both hungover—majorly hungover—so we decide brunch is in order. Pulling on a black and white stripe jumpsuit, I add my black fedora hat—since my hair is a mess—and my ankle boots. After applying some lip gloss, I meet Eden in the living room and pull on my coat. We link arms and head out to the waiting Uber, who drives us to Navy Pier. We climb out and as we are walking toward the cafe, someone yells out my name. Spinning around, I come face-to-face with Jennifer Dicks. She's from Collinsville, and I immediately freeze because I know when she returns home, Mother and Daddy will know where I am. "Jenny," I sweetly say when I realize she's staring at me. "What are you doing in chilly Chicago?"

"Business meeting. What are you doing here? And look at your hair, copper really suits you." Her voice is laced with disdain, she never did like me, not since Nick Amell took me to senior prom and not her.

"Thanks," I say, as I twirl the ends of my hair around my finger, the brightness of the copper a stark contract against my pale skin. "Felt like a change and thought, I only live once." I shrug nonchalantly as I say this. Not wanting to chat, I add, "It's great to see you, but we have a reservation."

Before she can reply, I link arms with Eden and we make our escape. With each step we take away from Jenny, my chest tightens. Breathing becomes difficult.

"Faith, babe, are you okay?"

Eden's voice is laced with concern. When I look at her, I see worry etched on her face. "I'm fine," I say, taking a deep breath, calming myself down. "Jenny and I don't get along, was just a shock seeing her." She eyes me suspiciously and thankfully doesn't probe any further. "Let's eat, I'm starving," I say, once again linking my arm with hers and walking toward the cafe which overlooks Lake Michigan.

We are seated immediately and I order a mimosa. I need the alcohol to calm my nerves. My mind is elsewhere all throughout brunch, I feel bad for Eden that I'm not one-hundred-percent here, but she doesn't seem to notice, she's too busy flirting with the gentleman at the table next to us. As we are leaving, he approaches and asks her to stay. I say a silent thank you as I want to be alone to process everything. After reassuring her I'm fine to get home on my own, I leave her with her new friend and make a beeline for the exit.

As soon as I step inside our apartment, I race to my bedroom and throw myself onto the bed and begin to cry. I knew my happiness wouldn't last. I knew eventually I would be found, that someone would find me. Now that it's happened, it's just a matter of time before Mother and Daddy show up. When they do, all hell is going to break loose and they'll demand I return to Collinsville with them and when that happens, I don't know what I'm going to do. I don't want to go home, I'm finally happy here. I've finally found love and I don't want to give that up. I just don't.

KEETON

I'VE JUST FINISHED READING THROUGH THE FINAL CONTRACT WITH A new company when there's a knock at my office door and in walks a grinning Blair, behind him a hesitant looking Faith.

"Hey," I say, as I stand up and walk around my desk. Walking over to Faith, I give her a welcoming kiss.

"I love that I get two hello kisses," she replies, as she wraps her arms around me for a hug. She seems different, something is up.

"You okay?" I say, as I pull back and stare at her. She looks washed out and tired. "Are you getting sick?"

She shakes her head, "No, yes, I don't know. I've just missed you guys, this is the longest we've gone not seeing each other since this all began. I was happy to get Blair's call and an invite for lunch."

My head snaps to Blair's and before I can say anything, he raises his hand. "I sent Barb out on an errand and snuck Faith in."

"Sneaky sneaky."

"Yeah, but Barb may be pissed when she gets back," he hesitantly replies.

"What did you do?"

"I umm, ahh—"

"Blair," I warn.

"It's nothing too bad. I just sent her to Bennett's house, saying that he and Stacey needed help."

"But Stacey's still in hospital."

He shrugs. "She doesn't know that."

A laugh escapes me, "Dude, you are so dead when she gets back."

"Hey, we get to see Faith, so any punishment will be worth it."

"You are terrible, Blair Schaffer," Faith teases, as she pushes me back so I fall onto the sofa. She straddles my thighs and kisses me. Gently grinding herself on my growing cock. As Blair steps in behind her, she drops her head back and gazes up at him. He lowers his head down and kisses her. I take the opportunity to play with her breasts that are at eye height. She moans and the sound heads straight to my cock.

"As much as I would love to stay," Blair says, "I'll go pick up lunch, while you two have a pre-lunch snack." With a wink he walks out. This will be one of few times I have been alone with Faith. It's generally the three of us together, but occasionally we get her to ourselves, and I have to say, I cherish these rare one-on-one moments.

Faith turns her attention back to me and she smiles. It's a

smile that shoots right to my heart…and cock. "Hey," I huskily respond.

Which Faith answers by pressing her lips to mine. Her tongue seeks access to my mouth and I willingly open. Sliding my hands around her back, I pull her into me, deepening our connection. Gripping the hem of her blouse, I lift it over her head, our lips briefly separating as the material passes by. Once free, she wraps her arms around my neck and deepens the kiss, gyrating her hips on my cock, which is now painfully hard and pressing against my dress pants.

Sensing my discomfort, she shimmies back on my thighs and makes quick work of popping open the button, lowering my zipper, and freeing my cock. The tip glistening with my arousal. She swipes the tip and brings her finger to her lips. Standing up, she pulls her jeans down but they get stuck on her boots. Not wanting to waste a moment, I pick her up and lower her to the sofa. Standing above her, I stroke my cock a few times before grabbing a condom from my pocket and sliding it on. While I'm doing this, Faith begins to flick her clit. Her eye locked on mine as she fondles herself.

I can't waiting any longer, I pull her into standing position and slam my lips against hers for a rough yet tender kiss. Breaking the connection, I spin her around, pushing on her lower back so her ass is in the air. Gripping her hips, I guide her back onto my throbbing cock. We both moan as her walls clench my shaft. Thrusting my hips back and forth, we moan and groan as pleasure envelops us.

My office door opens and in walks Blair, smiling when he sees us. Placing the food bags on the coffee table, he walks around the sofa and watches as I continue to slide in and out of her. Faith beckons him over with her finger. In between moans she pants, "Cock. Mouth. Now."

Not wasting a second, Blair whips out his semi-hard cock

and gives it a few strokes before feeding it to Faith. She sucks on his cock and it unleashes a gush of wetness. "You like his cock in your mouth as I fuck your pussy, don't you?"

She mumbles something, but with Blair's cock in her mouth it comes out all muffled. We fall into sync, my cock sliding in and out of her pussy in time with Blair cock slipping in and out of her mouth. Her walls tighten around me and she moans as her orgasm detonates. Seeing her climaxing sets me off, and I come with a guttural groan. Soon after, Blair comes too. She swallows every last drop of him before collapsing onto her stomach on the sofa. The only sounds in my office is the three of us panting.

"I'm…that…I have no words," she breathlessly replies.

"We should do lunch like this more often," Blair says, as he pulls his pants up, jumping onto the sofa next to Faith, who is still collapsed in a heap.

"I think we wore her out," I tease, as I remove the condom and pull my pants up. "Come on, babe, I'll show you to my private bathroom."

Picking up her shirt, I bend down and help her up. Her legs are jelly, once she's stable, I escort her into the bathroom. Leaving the door ajar, I turn on the faucet and run a cloth under the tap, then I step to Faith and wipe between her thighs. Her eyes are locked on mine as I clean her up.

"Blair Schaffer," Barb shouts as she storms down the hallway to my office, her shoes clicking on the floorboards. Faith's eyes pop wide open. "We're busted," she whispers. I lift my finger to my lips and mimic 'shhh.' She nods and I leave her to see what's going on in my office. Closing the door behind me, I walk in to see Barb berating Blair and an amused Bennett standing in the doorway.

"What's going on?" I say, hoping to defuse the bomb that is Barb Berthelsen.

"What's going on here, is that this fool here sent me to

Bennett's to assist him and Stacey. I get there to find no one home. Calling Bennett, he informs me Stacey is still in the hospital and I'm not needed."

Looking to Blair, I shrug, this was his scheme, a plan I was happy to be a part of not five minutes ago, now, not so much.

"Chill, Barb," Blair says, as he stands up and throws his arm around her shoulder. "It's payback, my dear, for that time you got me to go to Navy Pier."

She laughs and raises her hands in surrender. "Fine, truce. We are even. But, Blair, don't ever trick me like that again."

"Fine." He rolls his eyes. "As long as *you* don't trick me again."

"Do not roll your eyes at me, young man. Now, because of your errand," she emphasizes errand, "I'm taking the afternoon off." Before any of us can say anything, she's storming out of my office, slamming the door behind her.

"Really, Blair?" Bennett scoffs.

"It seemed like a good idea at the time." He shrugs, taking a seat as he grabs the food bag and pulls out a Chinese container and digs in. With a mouth full of honey chicken, he asks Bennett, "What you doing here? How's Stace?"

"She's good. Should be home from hospital tomorrow."

"That's good. So why are you here and not there with her?" Blair asks, before stuffing his mouth full again.

"I wanted to grab my laptop so I can keep up with all my emails."

"Don't worry about that. Focus on Stacey."

He nods his head, and then sits down and lets out a sigh. "I was so fucking scared when that gun went off," he says, rubbing his forehead before resting his elbows on his knees. "Made me realize how much I want her. Need her. I'm not going to let her go."

"That's great, man," I say, slapping him on the back. "Have you told her this?"

"Not in so many words."

"Why not?" I ask, grabbing a bottle of water from the mini fridge and taking a drink.

"'Cause he's a pussy," Blair says, "Dude, man up and tell her how you feel. If this has taught you anything, it's that life is short. Don't waste a minute of it."

"When did you get so wise?"

His eyes dart to my bathroom door and I know why. "I've always been wise. You've just had your head up your ass and never noticed. Now, go tell her everything you just told us, and you can name your firstborn after me."

"I'm not naming our child Asshat," Bennett teases.

A laugh escapes me and I faintly hear Faith laugh too, but thankfully Bennett is too preoccupied to notice. Blair flips him the bird and he laughs at that. "Okay, I'm off to look after my girl. I'll be back next week. Blair, try not piss off Barb again and, Keet, do a better job of keeping him in line."

"Dude, I'm awesome but not that awesome."

"God help the woman you end up with," he says to Blair. "She will be one strong, tough, and sassy woman."

"She sure is," I whisper under my breath as Bennett walks toward the door.

He opens it and looks back to us, "Thanks for having my back, guys, and for the pep talk."

"Anytime," Blair says with a salute.

"We've got your back," I offer, walking over to the door, we do the one-armed bro hug and he leaves. Closing the door behind him, I lean against the wood and let out a sigh of relief. "That was close," I say, as I walk over to the bathroom and open the door. My mouth drops open when I see Faith has on nothing but my tie from the spare suit I keep here.

She walks toward me and pushes me back to the sofa, I drop down with a thud. Blair scoffs, "What the fuck?" Then I'm sure his mouth drops open wide when he finally notices what Faith is wearing, or not wearing, I should say.

For the rest of the afternoon, we have a closed-door meeting, just the three of us and I can say, it's the best, most sexy meeting I have ever had in the office.

BLAIR

Life has been crazy these last few weeks, but now that Stacey is on the mend and back at work, life is starting to settle down. Things with Faith are still going strong, and it's perfect in every kinky way. The connection I feel when I'm with Keeton and Faith is indescribable, and I'm not sure my heart will handle it if this goes tits up. For the first time in my life, I've fallen in love. I'm scared to admit it to them but I'm sure they feel it too. This pull. This connection. This unwavering desire for one another. I know they feel it too, especially after the conversation the other week when Faith thought we were seeing Stacey as well as her. But I'm scared to broach the topic, because I will be gutted if they don't feel the same way.

This unexpected connection is freaking me the fuck out, but at the same time, I want to see where it goes. I want my happily ever after and all that bullshit with them both. But what if I'm wrong? What if they see it as nothing more than kinky fun and not a forever thing? Do I risk opening my heart and getting it stomped on? Or do I keep my feelings to myself and just enjoy it while it lasts?

I'm snapped back to reality, when Faith touches my forearm. "Are you okay, Blair? You seem—"

"Aloof and off in la-la land," Keet interrupts. He sits on the sofa next to me, pulling Faith down in-between us. Like always when the three of us are together, she snuggles into my side and lifts her legs across his. She runs her palm up and down my arm with one hand and with her other hand, links her fingers with Keeton's. The three of us fit together perfectly and seeing this reaffirms what I feel, and I decide, 'fuck it,' it's time to brush the sand out of my ass and lay it all out.

"Guys," I say, my throat suddenly dry. My heart racing. Faith feels the tension in my body because she sits up and turns to face me.

She reaches out and cups my cheek. "Blair, babe, what's wrong?"

"I...umm, ahh."

"Dude," Keeton says. "Tell us what's wrong."

"I'm scared."

"Scared about what?" Faith questions, her voice laced with worry.

Looking to her, I smile but it doesn't reach my eyes. It feels forced. I hate seeing worry etched on both their faces. Taking a deep breath, I go for it. "This all started out as fun, but over the weeks, it's changed. It's...it's become, I can't—"

"Can't what?" Keeton snarls.

"I can't deny this connection any longer." Standing up, I sit on the coffee table and reach for their hands. Squeezing them, I close my eyes, "What we have is more than just kinky fun." Opening my eyes again, I flick my gaze back and forth between them before I quietly say, "I want more. I want a happily ever after and all the jazz that goes with it."

"Ohh, thank fuck," Keeton says, my eyes pop wide open at his declaration. "I've felt the connection between us changing too, Blair. I was worried that it was just me feeling this, so I never said anything to you or Faith." He pauses. "Blair. Faith. What do we do now?"

Faith sniffles and that's when I notice she's crying. "This unexpected connection means everything to me too," she sniffles. "You both mean more to me than I could ever have imagined, but if we take this further." She flicks her finger in a circle at us and swallows deeply. "Then I need to tell you about me. About the real Faith Robinson…Bailey."

FAITH

"You don't have to do this," Keeton says, "I don't care about your past."

"Neither do I," Blair agrees. "Unless you have a kinky video collection from your past, then that's okay to share with us."

A laugh escapes me. That is one of the things I love most about these two, they can make me laugh, even when discussing something serious. "No, no hidden collection, but maybe we should start one." I wink at him.

"Duly noted for later," Blair says.

"Video date aside, I need, no, I want to tell you about the old me." They both nod their heads at me. "So, as I was saying, my parents are Fleur and Arnold Robinson-Bailey, and what you've read in the papers is nothing compared to what it really was like living there." My mind drifts back to my life before…

…"Not like that, Faith," my mother scolds me, they are her four favorite words when it comes to me. It doesn't matter what I do, it's never enough for Mother. Never, in my life have I ever heard praise from her, but she has scolding me down to a fine T. I'm not good enough. I never have been and never will be, not in her eyes. Fleur Robinson-Bailey wears many masks, but a loving caring mother isn't one of them, unless we are in public that is. To the world we are a happy, loving family but behind the estate fence, we are anything but. Father hides in his office and pretends everything is fine. Turning a blind eye to mother's indiscretions in private, and in public, playing the authoritative attorney and happy family man. Trenton fucks anything with a heartbeat, male or female. My dear brother thinks the world owes him, and with his second chance, he's taking advantage of everyone, and everything. And finally, there's Mother. Fleur Robinson-Bailey is unlike anyone I have ever met before. People cower in her presence, they bow down at her feet and do what ever she demands. How Daddy puts up with her, I don't know but the fact he does must mean that her alleged affair with her secretary, Sonja, isn't true. What they fail to realize though is, everyone knows what really goes on behind the estate walls, but Mother and Father are so far up their own asses, they don't see that we are a laughingstock around here.

"Faith, are you listening to me?" Mother scolds me; again.

"Sorry, Mother, I'm trying."

"Well, try harder."

I roll my eyes and she sees. "Faith Bailey-Robinson, do not roll your eyes at me. Do you know what's on the line here if we don't come across as the perfect family?"

I wish I had the guts to say, well stop fucking everyone who isn't Father and we wouldn't have to do this…but I don't. I smile. "Sorry,

Mother." And before she can berate me any further, Father arrives and takes the attention from me.

"Arnold, seriously, why are you dressed like that?"

Father is wearing his usual three-piece suit. "I'm dressed how I always am and if you don't like it, then I can always leave." Wow, that's the first time Daddy has spoken to Mother like that.

"No," she snaps at him, "we all need to be here for this."

"Where's Trenton?" Just as father asks this, from the janitor's closet next to us we hear a guttural moan, followed by some skank moaning, "Harder, Trenton, harder."

Mother storms over to the door and bangs her fist. "Wrap it up, darling." A few moments later, Trenton and Mother's secretary, Sonja, emerge from the closet. Mother's eyes pop open, and if it weren't for the Botox in her forehead, her eyes would have risen in shock. Seems Mother and Trenton have the same taste in women. For the first time in weeks, no months, I genuinely smile at this revelation. Before World War Three erupts, we are called upon. With a smile on my face, we all walk into the room and Mother addresses the crowd, her fake persona slipping easily into place, and once again she becomes Fleur Robinson-Bailey: beloved mayor and hypocrite. And they lap up her lies just like they always do.

"It was at that speech I decided to leave, I couldn't take the falseness that had become my life anymore. I wanted to find the real Faith and live my life how I wanted." I pause and look at them, there's no judgment or disgust etched on their faces. They are just Keeton and Blair. "So yeah, that's me, the real me."

"We don't give a shit about that," Blair says. "All we care about is the you, from now. You are the sexy as sin, copper-haired vixen, who has brought so much to my and Keet's life." I can tell from the look in his eyes he's telling the truth.

"Faith, we know the real you." Blair nods in agreement to

Keeton's words, "Sweetness, we all have a past, it's a part of what makes us who we are today, and I can unequivocally say, I don't give a shit about your past. I care about the here and the now." He pauses and then looks to Blair, something passes between them. "Faith, we love you."

My eyes pop open at this declaration, it takes me a few moments to process his words. "I love you both too." I reach out and squeeze each of their hands, and then my gaze darts between them. "But what if they find me?"

Blair comes and sits next to me, he rests his palm on my thigh and squeezes. "We will deal with that if they do. If we can handle telling people we are a throuple, then I'm sure we can handle Fleur and Arnold Robinson-Bailey." He pauses, leans over, and kisses me. His kiss lets me know everything he just said is one-hundred-percent the truth; it really is how he, well they, feel. "Now, go grab the camera, we have a video collection to start."

Just like that, Blair and Keeton make all my worries disappear and we make one sexy as hell home video. We are blissfully happy, but the following day everything implodes in a spectacular way.

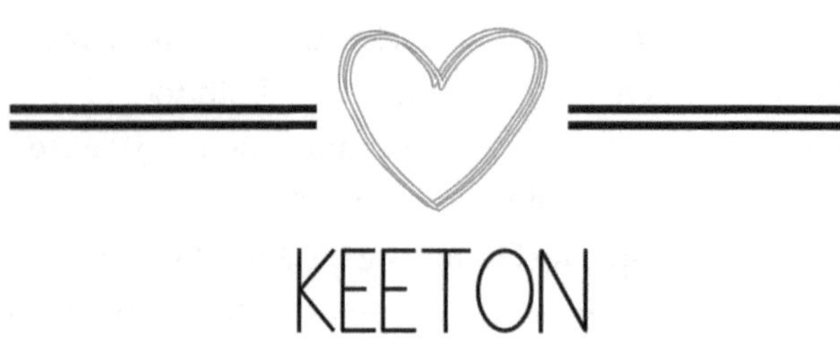

KEETON

When we wake the next morning, Faith is quiet and not herself. Don't get me wrong, she's usually quiet until she's had her coffee, but she's currently on coffee number two and unusually silent this morning.

"You okay, babe?" I ask, as I sit next to her on the sofa.

She nods but doesn't say anything. Taking the mug from her hands, she gives me the evil eye AND growls as I place it on the coffee table. Pulling her onto my lap, I wrap my arms around her waist and stare into her baby blues, which I notice are dull and lifeless this morning. Seems her confession from yesterday is weighing heavily on her. I smile reassuringly at her, my fingers tracing circles on her thigh. She shivers and relaxes in my arms, exactly what I hoped would happen.

Placing my finger under her chin, I tilt her face toward me. "Wanna try again, Sweetness? And this time don't bullshit me that there's nothing on your mind."

This causes her lip to lift in a half smile, but it doesn't reach her eyes. Seeing her like this worries me, dread starts to build in my stomach. "Are you sure you want to be with me, knowing who I am? Knowing who my family is?"

"Yes," I matter-of-factly state, not an ounce of hesitation in my voice.

"Really?"

"Really really. Faith, I don't care what your last name, well what your full, super-long name is. All I care about is you. The Faith I have fallen in love with. We all have a past, we can't change that. All we can do is focus on the now and the future."

She stares at me for a few moments. "When did you get so wise, Mr. Knight?"

"I've always been wise."

"Modest much?" she teases.

"Hanging around Blair is starting to rub off on me," I reply, shrugging my shoulders.

"What have I done now?" Blair asks, walking into the room after his shower.

"Your behaviors are rubbing off on me."

"Pffft, more like you are corrupting sweet innocent little me." Faith and I both burst out laughing. "Why do people always laugh when I say that?"

"'Cause you are far from sweet and innocent," Faith says, as she stands up and drapes her arms over his shoulders, "But it's okay, I love you anyway."

Blair leans forward and presses his lips to hers for a quick kiss. "And we love you too."

Standing up, I walk over to them. Pressing myself into Faith's back. Leaning down, I place a gentle kiss on her earlobe. Her body shudders when Blair kisses the other side in the same spot. Soon she is a wanton mess between us. With a slap on her ass, I declare, "Get dressed. We have somewhere to be."

With that, I walk away from them, to a chorus of, "The fuck?" and "Teasing asshole."

"Trust me," I throw over my shoulder. "We will pick this up later, but first we need to show Faith just what we think about her."

Blair's eyes brighten. "Yes," he hisses. "Trust us, Sweetness."

"I trust you," she says. "But you could at least give me an orgasm first."

"Delayed gratification," Blair croons. He places a kiss on the tip of her nose before stepping around her and toward me. As he reaches me, he whispers, "What was the plan again?"

Shaking my head at him, I ask, "Seriously, you've forgotten already?"

"Sue me. I saw Faith and everything went poof. Not my fault she has that effect on me."

I can't fault him for that, but I'll never admit it to him. "I see her, I still remember."

"Ohh, my apologies, oh mighty 'I remember everything' one." He hails toward me as he says this.

"You're forgiven," I tease, "Now hurry up, we leave in ten."

***

"Oh My God," Faith gushes. "That was amazing."

The amazing she is referring to is indoor skydiving at the iFLY in Lincoln Park. The three of us partook in two flights each. Mister 'I'm Awesome' didn't enjoy it too much, and Faith and I have been teasing Blair all afternoon.

We stop at a bar and grab a few beers and some snacks since we missed lunch. Blair is still kinda pale. "Aww, does Blair still got a queasy tummy?" Faith teases. "Do you need Faith to kiss you all better?"

"A kiss might help," he sadly replies. I roll my eyes and shake my head at Blair being a baby, but he seems to have Faith wrapped around his little finger. She leans across the table and presses her lips against his. Giving me a perfect view of her fine ass encased in her jeans that look like they were painted on. Their kiss quickly turns heated but she pulls back, pecking him on the tip of his nose. "There all better," she seductively whispers, as she takes her seat again.

Placing my beer on the table, I look to Faith, sliding my hand up her thigh. "I think I'm starting to feel ill now."

"We cannot have that." She leans over to me and presses her lips to mine. Threading my fingers into her locks, I gently tug as her tongue slips into my mouth. Pulling her to me, I deepen the kiss. When she pulls back, her eyes are hooded. Her breathing erratic. Winking at her, I pick up my beer and take a sip.

"Come on, we have to get home and ready for tonight," I say.

Neither one make a move to finish their drinks, after draining mine, I look between Faith and Blair. "If we hurry, we might have time for a kinky fun shower before we go."

That sparks something in each of them, I have never seen them drink their beers so quickly. Thirty minutes later, we are back at Blair's place. Within five seconds of walking inside, we are naked and wet in the shower together.

We spend a good hour or so in the bathroom, ravaging Faith. Each of us taking a turn at fucking Faith. Once we are spent, we finish showering before getting dressed for the night ahead, celebrating the nuptials of Bennett and Stacey.

"So, just to get this straight, Bennett and Stacey got hitched in

Vegas after Bennett's ex shot Stacey. And they met when a package was misdelivered to her office."

"Yep," I say, as I do up the last button on my shirt.

"Do they know we're a throuple?"

"No," I say shaking my head.

"So tonight is our coming out party, as such?"

"Yep."

"Don't you think we should chose a night that's not so important?"

"No. I want to show you off to the world," I say, as I slip on my shoes.

"But it's their belated wedding reception," she says.

"So?"

"So, it should be their night."

"Faith, no one is going to care about me, you, and Blair. Trust me."

"Why are we trusting you?" Blair says, stepping in from the closet and fastening his cufflinks.

"Faith is worried us coming as a throuple is going to take the attention from Bennett and Stacey."

"Who cares if it does?" Blair shrugs, "I want to shout to the world that we are together."

"But it's their night," she pleads again.

Staring I her, I relent. "If you feel strongly about it, we will hold off sharing that we are a throuple. Choose one of us as your date for the evening and we will 'come out' at a later date."

"Thank you, I appreciate that."

"So who's your date tonight?" Blair asks.

"Neither of you. The three of us are attending as friends."

"Spoilsport," Blair scoffs as he steps to Faith. "By the way, you look fucking stunning."

Faith is wearing an emerald green cocktail dress that makes the copper of her hair pop and the blue of her eyes extra vibrant.

"Couldn't have said it better myself," I say. "Really wish we could show you off as ours." She goes to speak but I press my finger to her lips. "But we will wait. However, when we get home, you need to make it up to us."

"Deal," she whispers. As she turns to exit the room, she looks over her shoulder at us, and there's a gleam in her eye. "By the way, boys," she teases, knowing we hate being called boys, "I'm not wearing any panties."

She turns and walks away, leaving Blair and I open-mouthed…it's going to be a looooong night.

BLAIR

"HUH?" I ASK TOTALLY CONFUSED.

"Blair, I've seen the porn you watch, this is nothing compared to some of the shit I've stumbled upon you watching."

"Dude, that was one time and I clicked the wrong video."

"Sure, the wrong video." He uses his fingers to air quote and emphasize the words 'wrong video.'

"So it doesn't bother you that Keeton and I are both in a relationship with Faith?"

"Why should it?"

"'Cause it's not the norm."

"Define norm."

"One male. One female." I pause. Bennett doesn't say

anything, his silence prodding me to go on. "And what we have isn't the norm, we are two males and one female."

"Are you happy?"

"Yes."

"Then who gives a fuck?" he counters.

"Society."

"Fuck society," he declares, "If you guys are happy, then fuck everyone else."

"But—"

He shakes his head and waggles his finger. "No buts, now, when do I get to meet this chick who has your balls in her firm grasp?"

"Says the one who's handed his balls to a woman by running off to Vegas and getting hitched."

"I'm manly enough to say that Stace has my balls firmly in her grasp—"

"Or her mouth," I playfully add.

"Or her mouth. What I'm saying is, if Faith makes you and Keet happy, then go for it. Fuck everyone else." He pauses and stares intently at me. "Fuck them."

Before I can reply, Keet walks over. "What's up, assholes?"

"I was just teasing Benny here over the fact that Stace owns his balls."

Keet gives me a look that says, *'Well, Faith owns ours'* and then his mouth drops open when he hears Bennett add, "Just like Faith has both of yours firmly in her grasp."

"You told him?"

"No, he asked which one of us is fucking Faith, I stumbled and then he put two and two together."

"Don't you mean two and one?" Bennett says, his eyes darting between us and suggestively wiggling his eyebrows as he does so. *Cocky bastard!*

"You're okay with this?" Keeton questions.

He shrugs his shoulders. "Why wouldn't I be?"

"I don't know, it's not the norm for starters."

Bennett throws his head back and laughs, slapping me playfully on the back. "You two are so on the same page it's creepy. That's exactly what Blair just said, and as I said to him, fuck society. Fuck the norm and be happy. Now, bring her over, I want to officially meet the chick who has you both firmly by the balls."

Heading to the bar, I grab Faith. "Umm, I want you to meet Bennett."

"Okay," she says, eyeing me suspiciously. "What's wrong?"

"Ummm…"

Her eyes pop open. "He knows, doesn't he?"

"Yep." I let the 'p' pop. "He guessed when I stumbled over who you were here with, me or Keet."

She laughs, "Sooo, I…ummm…just had a similar convo with Stacey. Seems we aren't very good at hiding that we are a three."

We both laugh. Linking arms with hers, I make my way over to Keet, Bennett, and now Stacey. Their conversation halts as we walk toward them. As usual, Faith stands between Keet and me. It all feels natural as the five of us stand here.

"Soo, I'm Faith," she says to Bennett, offering his hand in greeting. "And congrats to both of you on your nuptials."

"Thank you," Stacey says. "I hear congrats are in order on your…"

"Throuple," I add. "Three in a couple."

"Ohh I like that, a throuple." Stacey adds, "And can I say, I'm so happy for you all. Oddly enough, this totally makes sense."

"Huh?" I deadpan.

"You remember the night Keet and I returned with burgers when you were working late?" Everyone except Faith nods. "I told the story of Kasey and Branson, and when you thought it was an incestuous threesome, you guys didn't bat an eyelid or choke like Bennett did. I didn't think too much of it then, but now, your reaction that night totally makes sense."

"I told them it doesn't surprise me 'cause I've seen the porn Blair watches," Bennett adds.

"It was one time," I plead.

Faith leans into me and whispers, "You'll have to show me sometime."

Seems her whisper wasn't as quiet as she thought, because Bennett laughs and shakes his head. "She's totally perfect for you two kinky bastards." He says with a smile, "Now if you'll excuse my wife and me, we have to mingle. Faith, it was lovely to meet you."

With that, he and Stacey leave the three of us alone. "Well, that went well," I offer.

The two of them nod in agreement, and then we all laugh. Seems we were worried for nothing, our throuple is strong and nothing can tear us apart.

FAITH

I am lost in my sexy kinky thoughts when Stacey strolls up beside me and asks point blank, "So which one are you dating?" Her question throws me for a loop and at my hesitation, she starts to laugh. "Oh My God, you're screwing them both, aren't you?"

"Ummm." My cheeks turn pink, giving my nonanswer away.

"Ohh, babe, don't be shy about that. If I may say so, you're one lucky chick." She steps to me and quietly whispers, "So, how does it work?"

Before I can answer, not that I know how to explain what we have to a stranger, she was called away. She leans in and whispers, "Later, I want all the kinky, filthy, sexy details." She winks at me before grabbing her drink from the bar and walking over to a stunning couple. She has jet-black hair and a prominent baby bump; her husband rests his hand on her belly. They are both beaming and make a stunning couple.

The hairs on the back of my neck prickle, and I look up to see Blair walking toward me. After finding out our throuple has been exposed, Blair and I grab our drinks and make our way over to Keeton. Who has now being joined by Stacey, and the stunning couple, Gage and Marlee, whom I'm introduced to.

There's no awkwardness as the seven of us chat and laugh. Conversation flows, the guys tease each other, like guys do. Then Bennett turns his attention to me, his gaze intense. "Faith, how the hell do you put up with these two?" As he waits for my reply, he wraps his arm around Stacey's waist.

I shrug my shoulders, my eyes flit to Blair beside me and across to Keeton who's walking back from the bar, drinks in hand for everyone. I am so in my head, happy with how the night is progressing, I didn't even notice Keet walk away. As I watch him walk back to us, I realize I'm unequivocally happy being with these two amazing guys. Sure, it's not normal what we are doing but it feels right. For the first time in my life, I'm following my heart and I've never been more content or free.

"Well, kudos to you. You deserve a medal or something."

"She gets us," Blair says, pulling me into his side and kissing my temple. "No greater prize than that," he smugly adds.

"Someone's damn confident of themselves," Bennett teases.

"Nope, just stating the truth."

"Truth about what?" Keet asks, as he hands me my drink, he winks and stands on the other side of me.

"Blair's confident of himself," Bennett says.

"Over what this time?"

"You and he being a prize for Faith."

"Well me, for sure, and Blair is a consolation prize."

"Consolation, my ass," he scoffs.

"Whatever the case," Bennett interrupts before Blair causes a scene, which I have found out he's prone to do with his antics. "I'm happy you guys are happy. And, Faith, you really are a trooper to put up with these two."

"Fuck off, asshole," Keeton scoffs. "Go feel up your wife."

"Don't mind if I do." Bennett removes his hand from Stacey's waist and squeezes her ass; she squeals and playfully slaps his arm.

"Stop it, Bennett. My dad is here."

Bennett shrugs his shoulders and places a gentle kiss on her cheek. You can feel the love and happiness radiating between the two of them. I find myself smiling because I have a love like that too. Only double because I have two men who love me like Bennett loves Stacey.

The evening flies by and before I know it, it's almost midnight. I laugh to myself when I realize the time.

"What's so funny?"

"Earlier I was thinking about being a princess and what happens at midnight."

"And what's going to happen at midnight?" Blair asks, his voice dropping to a deep timbre that reverberates through my body.

"That rather than turning into a pumpkin, I'll be turning into a wanton, panting sexual being."

"Taxi," Keeton shouts with a laugh. "What do you say, we whisk you home and see if your midnight prediction comes true?"

"Lead the way, Mr. Knight." Looking to Blair, I add, "Coming, Mr. Shaffer?"

"You will be soon," he smartly says, tapping me on the ass before linking our fingers together.

We say our goodbyes and then exit the same way we arrived,

me with my sexy men on either side of me. Tonight was amazing, beyond my wildest dreams actually. I'm grinning from ear to ear. Our 'coming out,' as such, wasn't as big of a deal as I expected. Everyone accepted us, no one judged or made snide comments. If anything, they were intrigued by us. I felt like a fucking princess, with two princes. I'm on cloud nine but it all comes crashing down when we bump into the last person I expect to see here.

FAITH

"Hello, Mother," I say, as her eyes roam over me from head to toe. I shrink down at her perusal of me, just like I used to. The look on her face is a mixture of disgust and disappointment; clearly nothing has changed in the time I've been away when it comes to the relationship between she and me.

"What have you done to yourself?" she asks in her usual condescending way.

"I'm fine, thanks for asking," I snarkily reply. *Wow, where did that defiance come from?*

"I didn't raise you to speak like that. And I asked you a question, what have you done?"

"I started living *my* life. For the first time ever, I'm living how I want to live. I'm happy. I'm in love. I'm being me, the real me."

Her eyes dart between Blair and Keeton, if looks could kill, they'd both be dead by now. "With which one?"

"Both of them."

She stares at me open-mouthed and in shock. First time ever I have seen her speechless. "You can't be serious, Faith?"

"Dead serious," I confidently say, lacing my fingers with each of them and gently squeezing. My heart is racing right now, I've never spoken to Mother like this before. From beside her, I see Daddy smile, but he quickly replaces it with his blank expression, one he has mastered over the years.

"Hi, Daddy," I say, dismissing Mother.

"Faith," he says, his tone void of any emotion. "How are you?"

"Fan-fucking-tabolous." I say, this garners a grin from him and a scowl from Mother.

"Come, Arnold," Mother snarls at Daddy, and like the good little lapdog he is, he follows her. She walks off without a good-bye. Daddy looks over his shoulder at me and winks before turning and chasing after Mother...just like he always does.

Shaking my head, a tear falls down my cheek, "Why does he stay?" I sadly whisper, as another tear leaks from my eye. Blair and Keeton sandwich me between them and I cry into Blair's chest. From behind me, Keeton whispers in my ear, "Come on, let's get you home."

Nodding sadly, I follow them out of the hotel. The joy of the evening evaporating instantly.

Before I know it, we are pulling up at Blair's house. Robotically, I climb out of the car and head inside, stripping off my dress, I fall into bed and continue to cry. The guys join me and hug me. No words are spoken but their gestures say everything.

"I love you both," I sleepily whisper.

"We love you too." Keeton whispers. They each place a kiss on my head, it calms me. My last thought before I drift off is I'm thankful to have them on my team.

The next morning, Blair and Keeton treat me to breakfast in bed. We don't discuss what happened last night, but it's there in the background, lingering like the pain in the ass my parents are. As we clean up the breakfast dishes, I broach the subject. "Soo, umm, last night…"

"Faith, no," Blair starts. "You don't need to talk about it until you're ready. We can see you're upset about it, and we don't want to make that worse."

"Babe," Keet adds, "Blair is right, I don't say that often,"

"Hey," Blair interrupts, garnering himself a glare from Keet.

"But in this case, it's true. You've told us enough to know that last night will be eating at you, but we also know, it must be hard for you seeing them again. When you're ready to discuss it, we can, but in the meantime, I think I know of a way to keep you distracted."

And distracted I was.

For the rest of the day, they keep my mind off Mother and Daddy and my body completely devoured. I love Blair and Keeton with everything I have, and I will not let anyone ruin that, especially not Mother.

A few days after running into Mother and Daddy, I'm at home with Eden since it's Taco Tuesday. The guys are giving me space to process the events of the last few days, but I'm secretly hoping they pop by. We've just finished cutting up the lettuce and tomatoes when there's a knock at the door. A smile graces my face as I walk toward the door, but when I swing it open, that smile drops when I don't see my guys there. Instead, my mother is standing before me.

"Mother," I tersely say in greeting.

As usual, her eyes roam over my body from head to toe. Normally I shudder under her gaze, but not today. "Seriously, Faith, what have you done to your appearance?" She reaches out and rubs my hair between her fingers. The copper is vibrant right now as I refreshed the color this morning. "Pierre will be able to fix this." She shakes her head as she steps past me. She pauses mid-step when she takes in the apartment I share with Eden. "I have no words for the conditions you are living in." She turns on her heel to face me. "The sooner we get you home, the sooner we can fix everything."

"I'm not going anywhere, Mother." I say, crossing my arms. This is the first time I have ever defied her, and I have to say, I feel strong and invigorated right now.

"No daughter of mine will slum it like this."

"Like you give a fuck about me, Mother," I vehemently spit at her. I've never spoken to her like this before and it feels great to finally stand up for myself when it comes to her.

"Language, Faith. A lady doesn't use words like that." Her eyes catch the frame I got yesterday; it has a picture of me, Keet, and Blair from Bennett and Stacey's reception the other night. The three of us are all smiling, love radiates around us. Mother glares at me. "Faith, you need to stop whoring around and come home. Think of what this," she swirls her finger in the air pointing at the photo, "will do to the family. If it gets out that you are with two men. It's not natural or normal."

"Pot meet kettle," I scoff in anger, my blood boiling right now. Is *SHE* seriously lecturing me on having my love life splashed in the news.

"Do not speak to me like that, I'm your mother."

"You maybe the person who gave birth me, but you are no

loving mother. You think of only yourself and your next fuck-boy...or girl." Her mouth drops open in shock at my outburst. "You think of you and you only. Always have and always will. How Daddy has stuck by you amazes me, and don't get me started on Trenton."

"Trenton has nothing to do with this. You know what he's been through."

"Of course you defend the golden boy." I say, shaking my head. "And yes, I know what he's been through, I was there. I was a part of him getting better. You act as if his condition, when he was younger, gives him a free pass to be an asshole now. He had leukemia, Mom. Had being the key word here. He's in remission." Her face twitches when I say this. "And he's in remission thanks to me." I tap my chest with my index finger. "I don't get any thanks for saving his life, all you focus on is him. Trenton is a royal fuckup, Mother, you and I both know this,"

"Ohh, I need to meet your brother," Eden says from behind me. I turn to look at her and I glare. "Sorry," she says, raising her hands in surrender and she slinks away back into the kitchen.

"As I was saying, I'm the accident you never wanted. You made me aware of that each and every day of my life. It got to a point where I wanted to end it all, but then I'd be letting you win. I kept hoping things would change, but they never did. Wanna know why I left?" I don't give her a chance to reply, I keep going because I'm on a roll now. "I left because I knew if I didn't, I'd end up like Daddy: a shell of myself and I'd become a 'yes' person just like him. For some unknown reason, he unequivocally loves you. He turns a blind eye to your affairs, well as much as he can when they are splayed all over the papers. The disdain you show toward anyone, who you feel is lesser than you, is disgusting. That homeless person on the corner has more integrity than you do in your pinky. I didn't want to risk becoming like you, so I left. And it's the best fucking decision I ever made. I found me. I found friends who like me for me and not my bank balance. But most of all, I found true love. For the first time ever," I emphasize ever. "I'm happy, unbelievably happy, and I'm not going anywhere."

"It won't last. Happiness and love never do." She pauses for effect. "Power on the other hand does. Power is everything and, Faith dear, I have all the power. You? You have nothing."

"Power falls Mother. And when it does, you are going to crash and burn spectacularly. I cannot fucking wait to see the day that happens. Now get the fuck out of my apartment, you are not wanted here."

"Don't test me, Faith."

"And don't test me, Mother. I'm done," I defiantly say, feeling good for finally standing up to her. "Just leave, and while you're at it, set Daddy and Trenton free too. They will be better off without you, I know I am."

Walking to the front door, I swing it open and wait for her. She walks toward the door and stops beside me. "This isn't over, Faith. You've played your hand, but you won't see me coming, no one ever does. I don't care that you are my daughter, no one messes with Fleur Robinson-Bailey and comes out on top. Mark my word."

"You don't scare me anymore, Mother." I stare intently at her, but on the inside, I'm a quivering mess. The confidence I had earlier is waning and meek lil' Faith is emerging again. We stare each other down, the air around as palpable, thankfully she turns and walks away before I crumble.

Slamming the door shut behind her, I collapse to my knees and sob. The emotion of our encounter enveloping me. "Ohh, babe," Eden says as she wraps her arms tightly around me.

Little did I know, Mother's departure would set off a chain reaction of events no one saw coming.

BLAIR

Wow, I'd heard stories and seen the news when it comes to Fleur Robinson-Bailey, but seeing her in the flesh the other night—fuck me sideways—she makes Chucky look like a cute little doll. I cannot get the encounter with her parents out of my head, and Faith has not been herself since we ran into them on the weekend. She's been quiet and aloof, not her usual bubbly, outgoing, cheerful self. If I'm being honest, her behavior is worrying me.

It's Tuesday so tonight she's with Eden. I offered to host Taco Tuesday at my place, but she wanted a night with her best friend. I'd give anything to see her happy again, so I stopped arguing and gave in...but deep down I want to lock her away and make her happy again. It was amazing how one minute, the three of us were flying high and floating and then we met her parents and everything came crashing down.

The phone on my desk rings and it's Barb from reception, "What's up, Barb?"

"Ummm, I have an Arnold Robinson-Bailey here to see you and Keeton."

What the fuck!

"Show him to my office, Barb. I'll call Keet."

"Sure thing, Blair," she says. I love her, she never questions the random shit that occurs in this office, and of late, there's been tons.

I quickly dial Keet's office. "What up, dude?"

"Arnold is on his way to my office with Barb."

"As in, Faith's dad, Arnold? Arnold?" he questions again, to see if I'm messing with him. I've been known to do that before, but unfortunately this time, I'm not fucking with him.

"The one and only."

"What the fuck?" he shouts down the phone.

"Yeah, my thoughts exactly. He wants to see us both."

"Fuck! Okay! Be right there."

No sooner have I hung up and Barb is showing Arnold into my office.

"Thank you," he hesitantly says to Barb and stands just inside the door. Keeton comes racing in, nearly bumping into Arnold.

"We didn't get to officially meet the other night, I'm Keeton Knight." He offers him his hand.

Arnold looks at it and then smiles, a smile that reminds me so much of Faith's. "Arnold Robinson-Bailey," he replies, placing his hand in Keet's.

Standing up, I walk around my desk and offer my hand too.

"Blair Schaffer. Please," I motion to the seating area in my office, "have a seat. Can I get you a drink?"

He shakes his head. "No thank you." He takes a seat on the small couch, I take the single chair at the end, and Keet sits next to him. "You probably both are wondering why I'm here."

"It had crossed my mind," Keet says, at the same time I say, "No shit."

My comment earns me a glare from Keet.

Arnold raises his hands in surrender. "I'm not here to cause problems. I just want to know that Faith is happy and okay." It looks like he wants to say more but he doesn't.

To say his words shock me is the understatement of the fucking year. "Why? Why now, after all this time? Doesn't seem like you care about her."

He shakes his head. "I care more than you know. More than I let on." He pauses and swallows. "She's my little girl. Not knowing where she was and if she was okay has been eating at me. But seeing her on Saturday night, with light in her eyes again, was wonderful to see. Was it a shock to hear she's in a relationship with two men? Yes, but I want her to be happy and clearly, she's found that with you both. I know you don't owe me anything, but I'd like to arrange to meet with her." He quiet silently adds, "I've missed her."

"Why now?" Keet asks, always the levelheaded one. "Why not look for her when she first left?"

"As much as I missed her, I knew she was better off away from Fleur." Both Keet and my eyes pop open at this comment. "I love my wife dearly, despite everything she does, but she's not maternal in any sense of the word. She never has been, and that's my fault. I'm the one who wanted children. I just didn't realize what my selfish need would cost them both. Faith leaving was the best thing for her. I know I wasn't the best father to her when she was older, but when she was little..." He drifts off and smiles, clearly remembering a happy time. "When she was little, she and I had a great father/daughter relationship. She was the happiest child, she'd follow me around. She was my little shadow. She'd sit in the office with me while I was working, and she'd pretended to work too, drawing and coloring. When Trenton got sick, that's when everything started to fall apart. I can't pinpoint exactly when it all went wrong, but I know I failed my daughter. When she left, I thought it was for the best." He looks between us. "And it was. This weekend, I saw her before Fleur did. She looked so beautiful and happy, my heart soared seeing her. I haven't been able to get the picture of her on both your arms as you were leaving out of my head. She was beaming, she looked like a princess with her two princes."

I stare at the man before me. I want to believe he's full of shit and here with ulterior motives, but I think he's telling the truth. He genuinely loves and misses Faith. "You realize she might not want to see you, right? The decision to see or not see you is up to her?"

He nods his head. "I understand. That's why I'm here talking you, I don't want to overwhelm her, but if I know Faith, she'll be up in her own head right now and she'll be shutting down."

So he *does* know his daughter.

"From the look on both your faces right now, I think I'm right. Look, we are staying at The Langham, Fleur has an appointment the day after tomorrow, with Trenton and his..." He pauses and shakes his head.

He's hiding something, I think to myself.

"That's not important, maybe she can come visit me then, we can meet in The Langham Club."

Without thinking, I say the first thing that's comes to my mind, "Go fuck yourself."

"Blair," Keeton scolds me. "This isn't our decision, this is Faith's." He eyes me in the say-another-word-and-I'll-kick-your-fucking-ass way. Sitting back in my chair, I shake my head as he addresses Arnold, "We don't promise anything, but we'll speak to her," Keeton assures him. "Give me your number, and I will let you know her decision, but ultimately it's her decision. Blair and I will not tell her what to do."

"Thank you," he says, "That's all I ask."

He stands up and hands me his business card, offering his hand once again. "Thank you for looking after my little girl." He nods at us and turns, exiting my office.

The door closes behind him and I look to Keeton. "Well, that went well," I say as I roll my eyes.

"You think that was tough, we need to speak to Faith."

"Tomorrow, let her enjoy Taco Tuesday with Eden tonight AND you need to tell her. Personally, I'm sticking with my 'Go fuck yourself' stance."

"He's her dad, Blair."

"Some fucking dad he's been."

"We all make mistakes."

"And he's made a colossal one when it comes to Faith."

"Well, the decision's hers."

"Yeah, yeah," I agree, and as I sit here and ponder everything, I wonder what Faith will do.

KEETON

The morning after Taco Tuesday, Faith returns to Blair's; he and I are working from home this morning. Knowing we have a tough conversation ahead, I thought us being here with her at home would be best. She quickly grabbed a shower and comes out in her satin robe; she's obviously having a lazy day.

Blair hands us our coffee, and with our drinks in hand, we sit in the living room together. Blair looks at me and give me the 'now or never' look. Blair takes the coffee mug from her hands, and like when I did it the other day, she growls and gives him a look that could kill.

She sees the look on his face and her gaze darts to mine. "What's going on?" she questions.

"Faith, babe, your, umm, ahh," I'm a stuttering mess right now, not quite sure how to broach this, "your dad wants to see you tomorrow morning."

"What?" she asks, her voice full of shock.

"He came to the office yesterday afternoon, wanting to speak to Blair and me, hoping we'd convince you to see him."

"I told him to go fuck himself," Blair says. "But this guy here," he flicks his thumb toward me, "said we'd speak to you."

Her gaze snaps toward me, I hold up my hands in surrender, much like her dad yesterday. Shuffling closer to her, I take her hands in mine, staring into her eyes. "I told him it was up to you. We are not going to pressure you or force you to see him. This has to be your decision, Faith. I'll support any decision you choose."

"And I will too," Blair reluctantly says. "But I don't think the fucker deserves an ounce of your time."

"How did he seem?" she timidly asks. Pulling her hand from mine, she nervously runs her fingers up and down her thighs.

"I think he's confused. I could tell he was genuinely concerned for you, though. If I'm truthful, I think he feels like he's failed you."

"Yeah, I agree," Blair adds, "He does seem to care about you. A fuckton."

"Funny that it took me leaving for his parentalness to kick in."

"He's confused, I feel for the guy." She looks at me shocked, guess she didn't expect me to say that. "What are you going to do?" I ask.

She shrugs. "I honestly don't know. He and I were never close at the end, but there was always this connection, this kind of bond. Guess it stems from when I was little and we were close. Mother always managed to ruin our special father/daughter moments when I was older, not that there were many." Her gaze drifts off for a few seconds, her expression forlorn. Then she shakes her head and is back in the present.

"I really think you should hear him out," I say again.

She nods. "I think you're right, but…"

"But what?" I question.

"What if it's a ploy to get me alone so they take me back to Collinsville?"

"I," Blair says, "I mean we, will not let that happen. We can go with you, if you like?"

"You'd do that?" she asks, completely shocked.

At the same time, we both say, "Yep."

"Really?"

Resting my hand on to of hers on her thigh, I squeeze it reassuringly. "Yes, we won't let you go alone. When you love someone, you stick by them, even when the times are tough."

"Especially when they are tough." Blair adds.

"Faith, we will never leave you alone. You're kinda stuck with us," I playfully add, squeezing her hand again to convey what I'm saying.

"Well, it's a good thing that I kinda like being stuck with you guys," she purrs, her eyes suddenly full of hunger. "I really, really like when I'm stuck in the middle." Her voice drops an octave as she says this. She stands up, spins to face us sitting on the sofa, and opens her robe. She's naked underneath and it seems she's aroused. Her nipples are hard and rosy, she swallows deeply as she trails her finger between her breasts, over her stomach, heading between her thighs.

Looks like work will be delayed for a few hours. Grabbing her wrist, I stare up at her. "Let me," I growl, as I grip her hips and tug her toward me, my face in line with her pussy. Blair stands up and steps behind her, he lowers the satin of her robe down her arms, dropping it to the rug at our feet. He tilts her head toward him and kisses her deeply.

Lying back on the sofa, I tug on her hand. She stares down at me, her gaze full of carnal hunger. Lust. Arousal. Need. She kneels on the sofa, throws her leg over me and straddles my face. I devour her pussy with my tongue and fingers. From my peripheral vision, I see Blair start to unbutton his shirt. He strips off his clothes and feeds his cock into her mouth from beside us.

Sounds of moans, groans, and pure ecstasy emanate throughout the room. Slurping sounds increase as my mouth and her body meld together. Like a chain reaction, one after the other, we tumble into orgasmic oblivion. Faith comes in my mouth. Blair comes down her throat, and I come in my pants.

Blair collapses down beside us. We shuffle around on the sofa to get comfortable. We lay together, our limbs entwined as we flick on Netflix and watch a movie.

A few hours later, I hop up and get some work done, I also e-mail Arnold and let him know we will meet him tomorrow morning as we discussed yesterday. He immediately e-mails back, stating he's looking forward to it.

When I finish my work, I strip off and join a still naked Faith and Blair, who are both watching Netflix.

Sometime later, we make our way into the bedroom and once again, snuggle together. Blair and Faith drift off immediately, but my mind is on the meeting tomorrow with Arnold. I'm not sure I trust him, but there was something in his eyes that tells me he loves Faith in his own way, and he'd like to have a relationship with his estranged daughter. My last thought before I drift off is that tomorrow, everything will change.

The next morning, Faith is a jumbled mess of nerves. Her hands are shaking, She drops everything she picks up. Sitting on the end of the bed in her underwear, she looks to me and says, "Keet, I can't do this. I'm too nervous but at the same time, I'm curious and want to see Daddy." She pauses. "Keet, what do I do?"

"I'm not going to tell you what to do," I say, as I walk over to her, cupping her cheeks in my palms. "But for what it's worth, give the man a chance. We can leave anytime you want, just say the word."

She nods her head, "Okay, you're right. Let's do this." She jumps up, ready and raring to go meet her father.

"We have one problem," I say.

"What's that?"

I flick my hand up and down her body, "I love seeing you in nothing but your underwear, but I think you need to put some clothes on."

She looks down at herself. "Shit." She races into the walk-in closet and, a few minutes later, she emerges in jeans that look like they were painted on and a black top that makes her hair and eyes pop.

"Fuck me, Faith. You are gorgeous."

Just as I say this, Blair steps in from the en suite bathroom. "Fuck, can't we just stay here instead? Faith, you have to be the sexiest woman I have ever seen."

"Stop it, you two," she scoffs. "Let's get this over with so we can come back here and fuck like rabbits for the afternoon and evening."

"Fuuuuck!" Blair groans, adjusting his cock as he says this. "It's gonna be a long fucking day."

Thirty minutes later, we pull up at The Langham—clearly the best for the Robinson-Bailey's. Blair helps Faith out of the car and I hand my keys to the valet. Lacing our fingers together, the three of us walk into the hotel, our heads held high, and our hearts racing. We head to the elevators and make our way up to The Langham Club, on top floor. Stepping out, Faith immediately see her father, she pauses mid-step. Then he smiles at her and with that one gesture, I feel all the tension and angst leave her body.

She drops our hands and makes her way over to Arnold. He looks nervous, but at the same time, he has the biggest smile on his face at seeing Faith. Blair and I hang back, giving them a few moments together. Blair and I make our way over to the bar. We order scotch for us and a mimosa for Faith. It might be before noon but alcohol is needed to calm the nerves.

The sound of Faith laughing snaps my head in her direction, and my heart soars at what I see. Nudging Blair, we both look over and see Faith sitting next to her father on one of the sofas. They both look happy, radiantly so. The nerves from earlier are gone and they are replaced with joy and happiness. I have never seen Faith look so carefree and relaxed.

Arnold receives a phone call, he excuses himself to take it so Blair and I take the opportunity to go over to Faith. We sit opposite her, handing her a mimosa as we take our seats.

"You seem happy," I state the obvious but I don't know what else to say.

"I am. Thank you for making me do this."

Blair shakes his head. "We didn't make you do anything, Faith. We're just here for moral support. We love you and we want you to be happy."

"I love you both too," she says, "and I'm deliriously happy right now, nothing can change that."

She looks up when Arnold walks back and her face drops when her eyes land on her father's. "Daddy, what's wrong?" she questions him, as he shakily sits next to her.

Reaching over, he grabs her hand and squeezes, a sinking feeling develops in my stomach. "That was Grant, your mother's new advisor. There was an accident. Trenton's in a coma and he's injured."

"And Mother?" Faith questions, her voice wavering.

"She…she." He looks up at Faith, and he is completely and utterly shattered. "She didn't make it." He shakes his head in disbelief. "Faith, your mother is dead."

FAITH

"COME AGAIN?" I SAY, AS MY BRAIN TRIES TO COMPUTE WHAT Daddy just said.

"Your mother is dead and Trenton is in bad shape." He pauses. "I need to get to the hospital to see him."

"I'm coming too," I say, shocking myself that I care about Trenton.

"Come on, I'll drive us," Keet says.

The four of us silently make our way to the elevators, down to the lobby, and outside. Keet speaks to the valet to bring the car around. Daddy wraps his arm around me, pulling me into his side. Wrapping my arm around his waist, I snuggle into his side…just like I used to when I was little.

The valet delivers Keet's car, he helps me into the back and Daddy slides in next to me. He and Blair climb into the front. "Which hospital, sir?" Keeton asks.

"Ummm, I don't know. Give me a sec." He pulls out his phone. "Grant, it's Arnold. Which hospital is Trenton at?" He nods his head listening. "Okay, Faith and I are on our way." He hangs up. "He's at Chicago Hospital."

Keeton nods and puts the car into drive. He pulls out and makes his way to the I-90. Twenty-five minutes later we pull up out front of Chicago Hospital. Blair climbs out with Daddy and me and Keeton pulls away to park the car. Lacing my fingers with Blair's, we follow Daddy into the hospital.

The automatic doors slide open and immediately I'm hit with the antiseptic smell of the hospital. I'm not a fan of hospitals, not sure why, considering I haven't been to them often. The last time was when I was thirteen and I had my appendix removed. That was an inconvenience for Mother, she never let me forget that... and that's when it hits me: she's gone. I stop walking and swallow deeply. "She's gone," I whisper. My eyes well with tears at the realization that Mother will never berate me again. She will never put me down. She will never roll her eyes in disdain at me.

"What's that, babe?" Blair asks me.

"My mom's dead," I mumble as the first tear falls. I don't know why I'm crying right now. It's not like we had a good relationship, but she is, no was, my mom. I'm sure at one point she loved me; maybe. Blair wraps his arms around my shoulders, comforting me as I cry over losing Mom.

Then there's another set of arms around me. Spinning around, I look into the concerned eyes of Keeton. "Mom's gone," I stammer through my tears.

He lifts his hand and wipes under my eye. "I'm so sorry, Faith," he says, as I rest my head on his chest.

Blair hugs me from the other side and the three of us embrace as I fall apart over losing Mother, and then I think of Trenton. Pushing away from them, I race over to Daddy who is talking to a nurse, trying to get information on him. Daddy wraps his arm around me, pulling me into his side. A small smile appears on my face, I remember hugging him like this often when I was little. He kisses me on the forehead, and that one gesture causes the floodgates to open and tears pour down my face like an avalanche.

"He's going to be fine, Faith," Daddy says. He kisses me on the head and hugs me closer to him. Nodding my head, I don't say anything as I continue to cry, wrapped in Daddy's arms.

Next thing I know, we are in a room and Trenton is lying on the bed. Tubes running everywhere, he's very pale, he almost looks dead. That thought causes me to sob again.

Arms wrap around my waist from behind and I know it's Keeton. Running my palm along his arm, I lean back into his embrace. My eyes locked on my brother. "He looks dead," I whisper. Then I hear the doctor, "Right now, he needs a transfusion and then we can assess the rest. Arnold, we are trying to find AB negative blood."

"I'm AB negative," I say, pulling away from Keeton. "I'll donate."

"That will help, thank you." He turns his attention back to Dad. "We are concerned about his low white cell count and with—"

"What?" I snap, "His leukemia is back?"

Daddy nods. "Yes, we are looking into a new treatment trial. He and your mother have been here for a few weeks, he was accepted and they have been prepping to begin treatment." Then Daddy and the doctor start talking about Trenton's options. I turn my focus back to my brother. He's so pale and it's not just from the accident; he's sick again.

Closing my eyes, I cover my mouth and choke back a sob. "Let me donate my marrow again," I quietly offer, my eyes still locked on Trenton.

The doctor and Dad continue to talk about Trenton's health. A little louder, I say, "Let me donate my marrow." Both of them ignore me, again, and they continue to discuss options for Trenton. "He can have mine!" I shout and finally, I gain their attention. "I'm happy to do it again."

"It's not that simple, I'm afraid," the doctor placates me. "We need to run tests to make sure you're a match an—"

Interrupting the doctor, I smirk. "I… Am…A…Match," I defiantly say, pausing between each word for emphasis. "I donated marrow to Trenton when I was ten. I want to do it again."

"We will need to follow up on that, and retest you to ensure everything is still compatible, but this could be great for your brother. Where was the original donation completed?"

Daddy and the doctor discuss the first time I did this for Trenton, once again ignoring me. Turning away from them, I walk over to his bed and take a seat, pulling the chair closer. Taking his hand in mine I squeeze. "Hey, Buttmunch," I smile as I say this. "Seems like I'll be saving your ass once again. I know our relationship went to shit, but I never stopped loving you. I hope after this, we can get back to how we were when we were kids. You and I always had fun together until she got her claws into you…" My mind drifts to when Trenton and I were close, after the first transplant we became inseparable. Then when he got better and went into remission, he started to change. He took advantage of his second chance and thought the world owed him. When he was fifteen, he really changed. He became the local football hero, that's when Mother swooped in. Molding him into the douchebag asshole dick he became. He wasn't the Trenton I knew and loved anymore; he became this Stepford version. Occasionally, I'd see the old him appear and we'd have fun, but the switch always flicked and he became douche asshole Trenton once again. I miss and love the old him, I always hoped the old Trenton would come back one day but to date, he hasn't emerged.

Lowering my head to the bed, I quietly add, "After this, the only repayment I will accept is for the old, fun, non-douchey, non-asshole Trenton to return."

"I'll do my best, Twiggy," he says, his voice crackly and dry. My head shoots up and I see him staring back at me.

"I'll hold you to that, Buttmunch," I tearfully reply, tears pouring like a river down my face. "And don't do that again, or I'll kill you myself." My eyes pop open when I realize what I said, it's too soon to be making jokes about death.

Trenton laughs, "Twiggy, trust you to go there so soon."

"You know?" I question, I thought he'd been unconscious all this time.

He nods his head. "Was pretty sure she was gone, considering there was a metal pole sticking out of her chest."

My eyes bug open again, that's not an image I want seared in my brain. "What happened?" I ask, curious as to what caused the car accident.

"Beats me. One minute we are driving along. The next we are spinning and then there was an almighty crunching crash. Glass splintering everywhere. Then we were stopped. I looked over to Mom and there was a pole through the back window and through her. Then something hit us again, that's the last thing I remember until I woke up here."

"Fuck," I mumble.

"Fuck, all right." Trenton looks over to Daddy, who is now standing next to me. "Hey, Dad."

"Hey," he says, squeezing my shoulder. His hands trembling. "Are you okay, Son?"

"As much as I can be." He pauses. "Sorry about Mom," Trenton sadly adds.

"It's not your fault."

"But I was with her, I should have protected her."

Daddy and I both say, "No!" At the same time.

"Trenton, this was an accident. Plain and simple. We can't dwell on it or lay blame. Accidents happen all the time."

We all nod, the room silent except for the beeping of the machines connected to Trenton. He looks behind us, turning my head I see Keeton, Blair, and Eden standing in the doorway. When my eyes land on my guys, a calmness washes over me and I know that with them by my side, everything is going to be okay.

"Who the fuck are you people?" Trenton scoffs.

"Trenton," I growl. "That's Keeton, Eden, and Blair."

"And they are?"

"Cleary you're better, the assholeness is returning, they are my boyfriends."

His head snaps toward me and his eyes are wide with shock. "Boyfriends," he places emphasis on the 's' of boyfriends, "As in plural? As in two? As in threesome? A triad? A ménage à trios?"

"Yes." I nod with a smile. "We are a throuple."

"What the fuck is a throuple?"

"Three people who are in a relationship, a throuple," I say, as I stand up and walk over to Blair and Keet, scooting in between them and sliding my hands into their back jeans pockets.

"Who knew my sister was a kinky little minx?"

"We did," Blair whispers as he squeezes my ass.

"Stop it," I whisper.

"And who's the chick? Is she your lesbian partner?"

"Ohh, I like him," Eden says, as she walks over and takes the seat I just vacated. "I'm Eden, Faith's roommate." She glares at me. "And she failed to mention her brother was hot."

"Well, she never mentioned that she likes two dicks either," he counters.

"Trenton," Daddy interjects. "Don't be so crass."

Eden and Trenton begin flirting with one another. His face has a little color back in it now, and I think it has to do with Eden. I haven't seen either of them smile like they are with one another right now. Before I get the chance to tease them both, the doctor returns and explains everything that's going to happen next. I'm to be retested to ensure I'm still a match and once that's confirmed, we can proceed. Luckily for Trenton, he was prepping for the trial so he's ready to go. Once we are all up-to-date, the doctor leaves to check on when this will start.

"Thanks, Twiggy," Trenton says, "You always come through for me."

"It's what sisters do. You'd do the same for me, if it was me who needed you. You've always been there for me, Buttmunch, and vice versa." I know that last bit is a lie, well, for the last few years it has been. Recently, Trenton has only focused on himself. He knows it too, but we ignore that elephant and focus on the here and now. The past is in the past, we cannot change that. We can only look to the future.

BLAIR

"ARE YOU SURE ABOUT THIS?" I ASK FAITH FOR THE MILLIONTH time. For the past week, I've asked this question multiple times a day. Late yesterday, we received the news that she is still a match and they've set the surgery for today. I'm a bundle of nerves. Faith is lying on a hospital bed, ready to be whisked away for the procedure. She and Keeton are cool and calm, me? I'm a nervous Nelly who is precariously close to tipping over the edge. I don't understand how they are so relaxed about this. I've watched *ER*; I know that shit goes wrong all the time. You come to hospital for a fever and you leave with no leg, okay, I might be exaggerating there, but I'm scared shitless right now.

Arnold, as he has asked us to call him, has gone to be with

Trenton. The events of the past week are taking a toll on the poor guy. I can't imagine going through what he's going through right now. Losing your wife suddenly, your son's leukemia returning, and then your daughter being the one to donate marrow. That's some hardcore shit right there.

"Sorry, what?" I say to Faith, I didn't hear what she said because I was in my own head.

"I said, are you okay?" She reaches for me and as always, I go to her. Sitting on the edge of her bed, I lie down and rest my head on her belly. She begins to rub her fingers through my hair. "I'm scared," I whisper.

"You think?" she cheekily says, while Keeton says, "No shit."

Lifting my gaze to hers, "How are you not scared?"

"I am a little, but I've done this before. It sounds scarier than it is and it will all be over in an hour or so."

"But—"

She presses her finger to my lips, "No buts, Blair. Everything will be fine."

"Do you really have to do this?" I plead.

"Yes, he's my brother."

"Stupid brother," I mumble. I take her hands in mine and squeeze. "If you die on me, I will resuscitate you just so I can kill you myself."

"I'm not going to die," she says. "Besides, I have far too much to live for now. You see, I have two amazing, sexy boyfriends who I need to keep in line." This causes Blair to grin. "I'll be back here soon, annoying the shit out of your sexy ass before you know it."

"Promise?"

"Promise."

Keeton is shaking his head from the chair beside Faith's bed. "You are such a pussy," he teases me and then he looks to Faith. "And thanks for leaving me with this whiney asshole."

"My pleasure," she replies with a smile that lights up the room, then in a deep husky voice, she adds, "Just wait 'til I get home, so I can show you both how much I love you." She waggles her eyebrows at us, but before I can say something smartassy in reply, the door to her room swings open and the orderlies are here to whisk her away.

Keet leans down and presses his lips to hers. "Love you." I hear them whisper to each other. Stepping to the bed, I hold her cheeks in my palms and stare into her eyes. "You better keep your promise to me."

"I will," she says with a smile. I press my lips to hers and kiss her longer than I intend to.

Pulling back, I wink at her before I stand next to Keeton. He knocks my shoulder playfully. "She'll be fine, dude."

"I hope so," I reply, as we watch her get wheeled out of the room.

...Twenty minutes later

Pacing back and forth in the waiting room, I'm anxious and I feel like I could throw up. I don't think I've ever been this nervous before. "Dude, something's wrong," I whisper-shout, "She's been in there forever."

Keeton looks at the clock on the wall. "Dude, she's been gone for twenty minutes."

"That's too long."

"Blair!" Keeton shouts. "The procedure can take up to an hour and a half. Sit down before you wear a hole in the floor."

"Fuck," I mumble, as I fall into the plastic chair next to Eden. Sighing emphatically as I do so.

Eden leans forward and looks to Keet. "Is he always like this?"

"Not usually, no. This is a first," he says, as he reclines back into the chair and crosses his ankles over one another. It's as if he doesn't have a care in the world. It's like he doesn't realize the woman we love is in there, with two massive-ass needles drawing out her bone marrow so she can save her brother, again.

"I've never had the woman I love have surgery before," I sneer, as I take another deep breath, hoping this will be the one to calm me—FYI, it wasn't the one to calm me.

"She'll be fine," Arnold states, as he walks into the waiting room and sits down across from us.

"How do you know?" I snarkily retort. I'm being a total asshole right now, but I'm scared shitless.

"Because my daughter is a fighter and she's done this before."

"Damn right she's a fighter," Eden adds. "What she's doing for Trenton, again, is amazing. She really is a gem."

A smile appears when I think about Faith and her big heart. She really is an extraordinary woman, doing this, even though she was on the outs with her family shows just how remarkable she is. "Yeah, she's got this," I say and finally I feel at peace with what's going on.

"I'm going to check on Trenton," Eden says, jumping up and walking out of the waiting room. I notice a pep in her step and look to Keet. "What's going on there?"

"You noticed that too, huh?" Arnold says, a grin on his face. "I think those two are smitten." He pauses and looks between Keet and me. "Much like you two are with my daughter."

And the invisible elephant that has been sitting in the room is now right in front of our faces. "Very much so," Keeton replies to him. "Arnold, I know it's not standard, but your daughter is unique, and therefore it's only seems fitting that she has a unique love too. Faith is exceptional in every way possible, she makes us both better men. That's what I, we, love about her."

Arnold looks to me and I nod in agreement. "I could not have said it better myself. Faith means the world to us, and we will do anything and everything in our power to make her happy."

"That's all I want. I only ever wanted her to be happy." He pauses. "If I'm honest, I'm glad she ran away from us. Fleur was, difficult, you could say. I don't expect you to understand why I stayed with her, but I loved her in a way I cannot describe. I think it's how you two love my little girl. All I ask is that you look after her. If you hurt her, I will not be held accountable for what I do to you both."

Shit, Daddy Robinson-Bailey is hardcore, but when it comes to Faith, we are like that too. "Sir, we promise to protect and love her with everything we have."

We silently stare at one another and process the conversation we just had. I'm seeing Arnold in a different light now. I think from here on out, Faith will have a good relationship with him. You could see how happy they were at the hotel earlier this week. It's crazy to think, seven days ago we were in a hotel covertly meeting with her father, and now we are in a hospital, waiting for Faith to get out of surgery. Thankfully, we don't need to sit and fret any longer because the doctor returns and says, "She's in recovery."

FAITH

"How you doing, Sis?" Trenton asks me from his wheelchair by the window, as I'm wheeled into our room after donating my marrow, which he will receive later today. Daddy managed to get us a shared room, guess it's a perk of being uber rich. I've never thrown that fact around, but right now, I'm glad he did. I'm a tad overwhelmed right now, my emotions are all over the place.

"I'm okay. A little sore but all in all, I'm good."

"Wanna try that again without the lies?"

"Marrowwise, I'm good. A little sore and nauseous from the drugs, but I'll survive. Mentally, that's another story."

"What do you mean?"

I let out a sigh. "It's all pretty overwhelming," I sniffle. "Last week, I only had Keet, Blair, and Eden in my life. Now you and Daddy are here and it feels different, good but different, and Mother is gone. I don't know how I feel about that. Most people would be devastated that their mother is dead but me, I feel indifferent. I don't feel anything." The first tear falls. "And that makes me a horrible person," I blubber.

Trenton wheels over to my bed and carefully lifts himself up. He winces as he sits down next to me and begins to rub my back gently, staying near my shoulders. "You are not a horrible person, Faith, you are far from that. As for Mother, you feel what you want to feel." He pauses. "If I'm honest, I feel like you do. I don't know how to feel. It's weird voicing that."

"Glad I'm not the only weird one."

"We are Robinson-Baileys, we were born weird."

A laugh escapes me at that, and I wince in pain. "Don't make me laugh, asshole, laughing hurts."

"I'll try my best," he says. "But I'm funny as fuck so I can't guarantee anything."

The door to our room opens and everyone walks in. "What are you doing out of bed?" Eden scolds Trenton, "Get back in your bed now, mister." She growls at him before escorting him back to his bed. She fluffs, yes fluffs, his pillow and pulls his blanket over him again.

"How you doing, sweetpea?" she asks me over her shoulder, her attention fully on my brother.

"I'm doing okay."

As I say this, Blair and Keet squat down in front of me. I'm lying on my stomach at the moment so looking up his hard.

"Hey, Sweetness," Keet says, kissing me on the forehead.

"Told you both she'd be fine," Blair says, winking at me and giving me that gorgeous smile of his.

"Yes, you totally schooled us," Keet deadpans.

Daddy giggles and then our eyes lock, he sadly smiles at me. "Hey, Daddy."

"Faith, how are you?"

"Sore but okay." I take a deep breath, "I'm sorry about Mother. Sorry, I haven't said it before now."

He shakes his head. "It's fine. We don't need to talk about that now. We need to focus on getting you two up and running again."

Now it's my turn to shake my head, "No, Daddy. We need to talk about her." I pause. "Your wife died."

"I know," he sadly says. "My Fleur is gone." A tear falls down his cheek, he quickly wipes it away. Reaching my hand out, I flick my fingers back and forth, hoping Daddy will take them. He takes my hand in his and squeezes. Blair hops up and Daddy takes his chair. "I know your mother was hard on you, but she loved you in her own way."

"She had a funny way of showing her love. But this isn't about me and her, this is about me comforting my daddy over the loss of his wife."

"Faith Meredith Genevieve Rose, you really are a remarkable woman." He cups my cheek and smiles at me. "I'm proud to call you my daughter, and it's no wonder you captured the hearts of two men."

We all laugh at that. "And you thought I was the sexual deviant in the family," Trenton says, breaking the tension.

The room is silent again.

"I guess I better get in touch with Grant to check her funeral arrangements, now that I know you two are on the mend."

"Daddy, Mother will have it all sorted already. She never left anything to chance, or up to you."

"That is true. But I do need to call Grant, I'll be back in a moment." He kisses me on the head and leaves the room.

Lifting my head, I look over to Trenton. "Is he going to be okay?"

He shakes his head. "I don't know. I've never seen him like this before. I thought he tolerated Mom, but it seems like he loved her unconditionally."

"Seems that way. Guess he knew her in a different way than us." I pause. "I remember him telling us stories of when they were younger, they seemed so in love. What I don't get is, how he can love her like that considering she had all those affairs? We were like the laughingstock of Collinsville."

"Love is a unique entity," Trenton says. "You of all people should know that."

"True."

Tiredness hits me and I close my eyes for a moment, but clearly it's longer than a moment, because when I open my eyes again, the room is dark, except for a light above each of our beds. I notice Eden is snuggled in bed with Trenton. Daddy is on a recliner under the window, and my two guys have their heads resting on my bed.

Letting out a sigh, I wake Keet with my louder than expected exhale, his gray-blue eyes stare at me lovingly. "Sorry to wake you," I whisper in a hushed tone.

"You didn't. I was just dozing."

"Liar, I can hear it in your voice. You get this husky timbre to it when you first wake up."

"Do I, now?"

"Yep."

"How you feeling?" he asks me.

"I little stiff. Wishing I could lie on my back or side…and I really need to pee."

"Want some help?" he offers.

"I can't ask you to help me pee."

"You're not asking, I'm offering."

I stare at him. "Then yes, please, can you help me pee?"

"Helping," and he air quotes helping, "to pee, now that's a little kinky, even for us," Blair teases.

"You're a dick," Keet says, as he stands and helps me up and off the bed. I wince a few times, but all in all, I feel okay. Once my feet are steady on the floor, I stand between them. They both help me into the en suite bathroom where I pee, in a nonkinky way since I make them face away from me. Sure they have seen me naked, but seeing me pee, now that's whole new level. I don't think I will ever be ready for that to happen.

After wiping and flushing, I shuffle over to the sink and stare at my reflection. "Ugh," I groan in disgust, "I look like horseshit."

"You look beautiful to me," Keeton says.

"I agree, you are totally rocking this hospital gown," Blair croons, as he nuzzles my neck.

My body shivers in the most delicious way. My eyes close and my head drops to the side, giving Blair full access to my neck. "You tell lies," I whisper.

"Look at me," Keeton growls. My eyes pop open and, through the mirror, I stare into his gorgeous gray-blue eyes that are currently watching me intently; I shiver at the intensity of his gaze. "You are the sexiest woman alive, Faith. Don't ever think or say anything different. Otherwise…"

"Otherwise what?" I pant.

"Otherwise we will have to fuck sense into you."

"I'm down with just fucking," I cheekily reply, biting my bottom lip at the thought of them taking me right now.

"As much as we'd love to," Blair says, staring at me in the mirror, "you just had minor surgery. Fucking will have to wait and trust me, Sweetness, it will be worth the wait."

"It's always worth it," I say, "Everything with you guys is worth it."

"Once again, I agree," Keeton says. "Now let's get you back to bed."

We shuffle back into the room and this time, my two guys climb into bed with me, and the three of us snuggle in the tiny hospital bed. Me sandwiched between the two men who mean everything to me and whom I love with every fiber of my being.

KEETON

...Six weeks later

"I'M GONNA MISS LIVING WITH YOU," EDEN TEARFULLY SAYS.

"I'm gonna miss you too, babe, but you'll have Trenton to keep you company." Faith tearfully replies as she and Eden hug once again. Since her mom's death, the accident, and the surgery, Trenton and Eden have connected in every way possible. Seems Faith's donation helped Trenton immensely. His counts are up, almost back to normal, and it allowed him late entry into the trial. So far, it all seems to be going well for him and fingers crossed, he will be around to annoy everyone for a long time to come.

Faith's relationship with both her father and brother has changed it's dynamic. Seems Fleur was toxic to them all, and now that she's no longer here, everyone is getting along swimmingly.

The same can be said for Faith, Blair, and me. The three of us are officially moving into Blair's. We pretty much spend all our time at his place anyway, so it was the most logical decision. And since we decided, things between us have been great. The three of us have always had an intense connection but in the last few weeks, it's intensified immensely.

It all changed the night, we took our relationship to a new level…

…Faith is being all coy. It's been two weeks since her bone marrow donation, and two weeks since we have had any kinky fun. I think from the look in her eyes, that will all change tonight. She has sent Blair and me off with Bennett for the afternoon, promising us an evening we will never forget.

A few hours later, we return to Blair's. The house is dark but when we open the door from the garage, there are rose petals on the floor, leading us into the house. Looking to Blair, he shrugs and we follow the petals. Crossing through the living room, we enter Blair's bedroom. There are candles everywhere and on the bed is Faith. She's lying across the end, her back to us. She's hasn't turned around yet, my eyes roam over her sexy naked body, and that's when I notice it. Poking between her ass cheeks is a plug. Seems tonight is the DP night. We've never broached that but I have to say, it's been on my mind for weeks.

"Faith," I huskily growl, "What's in your ass?"

Finally, she looks over her shoulder toward Blair and me. "What, this?" she playfully teases, and she pulls her cheek to the side and bends her top leg, showing us everything. Not only does she have a plug in her ass, but her lips are smooth and glistening. She's already aroused and we haven't even touched her yet.

Quicker than the flash, Blair and I are naked, stalking toward the bed. My heart is rapidly beating right now. I've thought about taking Faith's ass on so many occasions, but it never felt right. But now, now it seems it's the perfect time.

Kneeling on the end of the bed, I lean down and place a kiss on her ass cheek. She shivers under my touch, tracing my finger up her spine, I notice Blair is kissing her. She breaks the kiss and looks over her shoulder toward me. She winks at me, lowering my head down I place my lips against hers. She pulls back and smiles at me. It shoots straight to my cock, "Hi," I huskily whisper.

"Hey. Enjoy your afternoon?"

"Not as much as I'm going to enjoy my evening. Seems you are—"

"—a fucking sexy minx," Blair interrupts, "Who is about to feel pleasure like never before."

Blair is now sitting on the bed, his back resting against the headboard. He beckons Faith to him with his finger. She lifts herself too all fours, giving me a spectacular view of her ass as she crawls up Blair's body. She kisses and sucks his cock before kissing up his chest.

"Hi," she whispers, pressing her lips to his.

"Sit on my cock, Faith," he growls. "Slide my dick inside your pussy and ride me. Get yourself so wet that Keet's cock will glide ever so easily into your tight sexy ass."

She moans and does exactly what Blair commands. My hand grips my cock and I pump up and down as I watch Faith ride Blair.

Faith looks over to shoulder toward me. "Please," she begs.

"With fucking pleasure."

Climbing onto the bed, I shuffle behind her. She's still riding Blair, I kiss and nuzzle her neck. Massaging her breast, she drops her head back onto my shoulder. "Fuck my ass," she whisper-moans.

Sliding my hand down her back, I palm her ass cheek and squeeze.

Tapping the tip of the plug, she moans, "Fuuuuck!" Gripping the end, I slide it out and slip two fingers in, scissoring them to stretch her just a little more.

Blair hands me a bottle of lube; I pour some on my dick and line myself up at her opening. "Please," she whimpers again. Ever so slowly, I slide my shaft into her. It's so tight, she tenses and I stop pushing.

"Relax," I murmur into her ear, immediately she does and I slide my dick the rest of the way in. Once my balls are pressed against her ass, I give her a moment to get use to having a dick in both holes.

"Please," she moans. Gripping her hips, I begin to thrust. And fuck me, being in her ass is the best feeling in the entire fucking world. I thrust in as Blair's dick slides out. We fall into a rhythm.

In.

Out.

Moan.

Groan.

Each of us spellbound by the pleasure enveloping us.

Faith's body stills between us and she lets out a guttural scream as her orgasm detonates. Hearing her lost in the ecstasy pushes Blair and I over the edge, and we come in unison. I come harder than I've ever come before.

We collapse to the mattress, a panting entangled mess.

A few minutes later, Faith's voice breaks the quiet, "I vote we do that again. I have never felt pleasure like that before."

"I concur," Blair says. "I don't think I have ever come that hard before."

A laugh escapes me. "I was thinking that as I was coming down from the high."

"I love our throuple," Blair mumbles.

"Me too," Faith murmurs, while I just nod.

Best. Fucking. Night. Ever.

• • •

A smile graces my face as I remember that night, and now that the three of us are moving into Blair's place, I'm sure we will have many more kinky amazing fun nights like that...now and forever.

EPILOGUE

Blair

The connection between the three of us is one I never expected, it was unexpected and not what I was looking for, but Faith and Keeton are my missing pieces. Separate, we are great people but as a throuple, we are amazing. Our connection and love is one I will cherish for the rest of my life.

Keeton

The connection between the three of us is magical in every sense of the word. They say the best things come in pairs, but when you have a connection like Faith, Blair, and I do, three is magic number, and it's now my favorite of all the numbers.

Faith

The connection between the three of us was just what I needed. Who knew prim and proper Faith Robinson-Bailey would end up with an unexpected connection like this? But now that I've found it, I'm never letting it go. Now that we are living together, I cannot wait to explore this connection further. Who knew that two plus one equals forever?

falling for DR. KELLY

They say opposites attract and Avery Evans is my polar opposite in every way.

She's quiet, reserved, and ohh so shy. There's something about this gorgeous school teacher I can't stay away from.

Doctor Flynn Kelly is sexy as sin, headstrong, and confident, but underneath his outgoing exterior, he's incredibly sweet and charming. He brings out a side of me, I never knew existed.

We are drawn together like magnets.

It's explosive.
Earth-shattering.
Out of this world.

When a devious rival tries to tear us apart, our differences really show.

Can two opposites fight the laws of attraction?
Or will our chemistry sizzle and burn out?

Read on for a sneak peek at Falling for Dr. Kelly…

Here is a sneak peek at Falling for Dr. Kelly, available now.

Baylor and I are lying under her bed giggling like schoolgirls. "That was awesome, BayBay. They had no idea it was me."

"I know, Avie, I know." Bay says with a smile that lights up her face. "We should do this again. It's so much fun playing each other."

"It sure is." I look to my twin sister and smile, happy that of all the people in the world I ended up with her as my twin. She's my BayBay.

"I love that you're my sister, Avie."

"And I love that you're mine too, BayBay. We are gonna be twinsies forever."

"What's a twinsie?" she asks.

"It's your twin, who is also your best friend," I explain to my older twin, by seven minutes.

"Twinsies forever," she whispers back. "Let's do it again and this time let's do it for a whole day."

"Yes, let's do it tomorrow."

As the memory fades and reality kicks back in, a sadness washes over me. Baylor and I were close and we swore we'd be twinsies forever, and up until recently, we were. She was one of my best friends, albeit selfish at times, but at the end of the day, she always had my back and I had hers. We were there for one another when we needed a shoulder to cry on or a hug just because. But she's changing before my eyes and turning into a horrible, despicable person. My BayBay, my twinsie, is wilting away and there's nothing I can do about it. This new Baylor is harsh and not a nice person to be around. She's always been the headstrong, outgoing, and brash twin, the complete opposite to me. I'm shy, quiet, and reserved. Some would say I'm a pushover but differences aside, we always had each other's back.

I want that Baylor back.

My BayBay.

I don't like this new one.

Today is my last day at Oasis, what I thought was going to be a sex-filled getaway didn't quite turn out how I expected. The first few days I hooked up each night but they were nothing to write home about, and then I met Paige Walsh. Paige is a smoking hot red-haired vixen and, rather than getting down and dirty between the sheets with her, we became friends. Platonic, no hanky-panky, non-kissing friends…and then she got back together with her fiancé and I really was relegated to the friend zone. If I'm honest, I'm glad Paige got her happily ever after, she deserves more than a weekend fuckfest with me. My dick, on the other hand, he isn't too happy with me right now. The term blue balls is an accurate description of my nether regions at this moment in time.

I just bumped into Paige and Cam, her douche fiancé—he

broke her heart and then game grovelling back, hence douche fiancé reference—but Paige is beaming right now. From the chats we had, he is the rum to her Coke and when he followed her here, it cemented her feelings for him. *Lucky bastard.* After walking away from them, I head down to the beach for one last swim before my flight home. Kicking off my flip-flops, I pull my shirt over my head, and drop my sunglasses on top of my shirt. Looking around, I see I'm the only one here, so I pull down my boardshorts and I run toward the ocean, naked as the day I was born. When the water is to my knees, I dive in, the water is cold and a shock to the system, but it's just what I need.

Breaking the surface, I shake my head from side to side, flicking water droplets around like a dog. Floating on my back, I stare up at the sky, it's the bluest of blue and there's not a cloud in sight. I'll be sad to leave this place, but after losing Paige—not that I had her in the first place—I think getting back to Chicago is what the doctor—me—ordered.

I really needed this getaway, the last few weeks at the hospital have been crazy busy. So busy I haven't even had a chance to hook up in the on-call room. It used to be great when Kristin Payne worked there. She and I had a mutual arrangement that worked for both of us. The sex was mind-blowing, there were no feelings or awkwardness; it worked great between us. Until she foolishly went and fell in love with her childhood best friend. But in saying that, I've never seen her happier. It was no surprise when she ended our arrangement. Was I sad? Sure, but I was happy she was happy. A few weeks later, he took a job in Australia and she left with him. Leaving me and my blue balls behind.

I've had enough with the moping, so I stand up and dive back under the water. When I break the surface, I swim until my arms hurt. I'm a fair way out from shore and if I'm honest, I'm impressed with how far I swam. Looking at my watch, I see I have to get back; otherwise I'll miss my flight. Swimming back to shore, I slip my shorts back on, grab the rest of my stuff, and head to my room where I shower and change for the flight home. While I'm in the shower, like I have the last few days, I pleasure myself to thoughts of Paige, wishing ever so hard it really were her. Closing my eyes, I imagine it's her hand gripping my cock and pumping. Squeezing the tip before sliding her palm down my shaft. My balls tighten and I come over the shower wall, murmuring her name as I empty my load.

Opening my eyes, I step under the showerhead, letting the droplets cascade over my shoulders, washing away the remnants of my self-love. Soaping up, I clean myself, climb out, dry off, and finish packing.

After checking out, I jump on the shuttle bus and it takes me to the airport, where I board my flight and head back to reality.

Preston Knight, my best friend and the best pediatric doctor at Western General, picks me up. "How was paradise?"

"Paradise," I forlornly reply.

"Why so glum?" I sigh, not sure what to say to him. "Dude, like seriously, what's up?"

"I have blue balls."

Preston laughs, a deep belly laugh which echoes through the car. I'm glad we are stopped at a red light; otherwise, I'm sure he would have crashed the car. "Are you telling me, Dr. 'I have an accent, drop your panties now' has blue balls?"

Nodding my head, I sigh dejectedly, "Yep."

"How? You just got back from a fuckin' adults-only haven."

"The first few days were banging—pun intended—and then I met this chick but she was…"

"Was what?" he questions, as he pulls onto the freeway.

"She was there after a breakup—"

"Rebound sex," he interrupts, raising his eyebrows suggestively.

"I wish. The ex-fiancé arrived. He followed her to Oasis and won her back." *Lucky bastard.*

"Well shit, so why not hook up with someone else?"

"I don't know. I just wasn't feeling it. After getting cock-blocked by her, I just, I don't know. If I'm honest, this weirdness goes further back. Ever since Kristin fell in love and moved to kangaroo land, I've just been out of sorts."

"Sounds like you need to get laid and you need to get laid good."

"Tell me about it. The boys are turning blue and I'm getting callouses on my hands from all the jacking off. I feel like a teenager again."

"If you like, we can go out tonight."

Shaking my head, I resist, "Nah, I need to get home, unpack, and get my head back into the game. Plus, I've got an early shift tomorrow."

"No worries, some other time then."

The rest of the trip to my place is silent. We pull up to my building and I climb out. Preston hops out and opens the trunk. Leaning in, I grab my bag. "Thanks for picking me up, man… and the talk."

"Anytime, you know that."

"Appreciate it. I'll see you tomorrow." Turning around, I head inside. The doorman, *he's new*, I think to myself, opens the door and nods at me. Nodding at the desk clerk, I push the button for the penthouse. The elevator arrives, I step in and the car whisks me up to my floor.

Stepping into my penthouse, I look around. It really is a bachelor pad, but it's MY bachelor pad. Everything is dark brown. My couch, the rug, the artwork. Hell, even the kitchen has chocolate brown granite and dark wooden cabinets. At least the walls are light, brightening the place up. As I head into my bedroom, I think maybe it's time to overhaul this place.

If I lighten the furnishings up, it might lighten my mood as well.

Dropping my suitcase off in the walk-in closet, I head back to the kitchen and pour myself a glass of red. I'm thankful I called my housekeeper and asked her to stock up today. Not wanting a heavy meal, I prepare a cheese platter and head out to the patio. I enjoy my wine and watch the sun go down. The sensor lights flick on and I realize I've been sitting out here for hours.

Picking up the empty plate and my wine, I head inside. Placing the plate and glass in the sink, I head to bed, hoping a goodnight's sleep will reset my mood, and I'll be ready to head back to work in the morning. I drift off to sleep and for the first night since meeting Paige, I don't dream of her. I take it as a good sign and that things will return to normal.

ACKNOWLEDGMENTS

Writing these never get easy…takes a sip of wine…here goes.

Thank you to my editor, **Karen** from **Barren Acres Editing.** I'm so grateful to have you on Team DL. You've been with me since the beginning, I couldn't image doing this without you. Thank you for everything you do, when we meet (and we will) the wine is on me.

Thank you! Thank you! Thank you! to **Dana Leah** from **Designs by Dana**. You NAILED this cover, it took us forever to find the right images but we got there in the end. I know I said Package was my fav but now, this one is. Thank you for bringing Blair, Keet and Faith to life.

As usual, a shout out to my beta babes; **Alana, Halle** and **Jenny** . Without you guys on my team, this would be a big old mess. Thanks for your feedback, guidance and support; especially in my first foray into ménage.

Thank you to **Ena** and **Amanda** from **Enticing Journey**. It's a pleasure working with you ladies. You made the release of this series so easy. I look forward to working with you ladies again.

Thanks to my hubby, **Troy** and my munchkins, **Piper** and **Kade**. You three are my everything. You make this authoring journey that much easier. Your support and hugs are everything. Love you guys long-time Xo

And lastly, as always, **you, my reader**. Without you guys, I wouldn't continue to do this. Your messages and reviews mean the world to me. From the bottom of my heart, thank you.

ALSO BY DL GALLIE

THE UNEXPECTED SERIES

When it comes to love, expect the unexpected

The Unexpected Gift

The Unexpected Letter

The Unexpected Package

The Unexpected Connection

THE CASTAWAY GROVE COLLECTION

Love has arrived in the Grove

Oasis

Unequivocal Love

Five Words

Broken Rules - coming mid/late 2020

...and a few more as well.

THE LIQUOR CABINET SERIES

Liquor has never been so disturbingly saucy

Malt Me (Book 1)

Tequila Healing (Book 2)

Wine Not (Book 3)

The Final Shot (Book 4)

The Liquor Cabinet: Series boxset

STAND ALONES

Out of Nowhere

Antecedent

Seven Nights

Falling for Dr. Kelly, a Falling novel

Falling for Dr. Knight, a Falling novel - coming May 2020

Doc Steel - coming June 2020

The Dirty Dozen: Alpha edition

The Rule Breaker Anthology - coming soon

In the Dark of Night anthology (only available in paperback directly from me)

Titanic Tales, a charity anthology (no longer available)

Gone Coastal, a sizzling summer beach anthology (no longer available)

Leave Me Breathless: The Lilac Collection (no longer available)

ABOUT THE AUTHOR

DL Gallie is from Queensland, Australia, but she's lived in many different places all over the world, including the UK and Canada. She currently resides in Central Queensland with her husband and two munchkins. She and her husband have been together since she was sixteen, and although they drive each other crazy at times, she couldn't imagine her life without him.

Shortly after her son was born, DL began reading again. With encouragement from her husband, she picked up the pen and started writing, and now the voices in her head won't shut up.

DL enjoys listening to music, drinking white wine in the summer, red wine in the winter, and beer all year round. She's also never been known to turn down a cocktail, especially a margarita.